★FINDING★
RUBY STARLING

★FINDING★
RUBY STARLING

KAREN RIVERS

ARTHUR A. LEVINE BOOKS

AN IMPRINT OF SCHOLASTIC INC.

Library of Congress Cataloging-in-Publication Data

Rivers, Karen, 1970– author.
　Finding Ruby Starling / by Karen Rivers. — First edition.
　　pages cm
　Summary: Through e-mails, letters, blog entries, and movie scripts, twelve-year-old Ruth, an American girl, and Ruby, an English one, discover that they are long-lost twins.
　ISBN 978-0-545-53479-6 (hardcover : alk. paper) 1. Twins — Juvenile fiction. 2. Sisters — Juvenile fiction. 3. Electronic mail messages — Juvenile fiction. 4. Blogs — Juvenile fiction. 5. Mothers and daughters — Juvenile fiction. 6. Adoption — Juvenile fiction. [1. Twins — Fiction. 2. Sisters — Fiction. 3. Email — Fiction. 4. Blogs — Fiction. 5. Mothers and daughters — Fiction. 6. Adoption — Fiction.] I. Title.
　PZ7.R5224Fi 2014
　[Fic] — dc23
　　　　　　　　　　　　　　　　　　　　　　　　　　　　　　　2014002269

10 9 8 7 6 5 4 3 2 1　14 15 16 17 18
Printed in the U.S.A.　23
First edition, September 2014

FOR KATE LEVANN, WHO IS POSSIBLY MY VERY OWN ENGLISH TWIN, EVEN THOUGH WE LOOK NOTHING ALIKE, ARE DIFFERENT AGES, AND AREN'T, IN FACT, RELATED.

Dear Ruby Starling,

I know no one starts off email messages with "dear," but this is more important than most email messages. It may even be The Most Important Email Message Of Our Time! ALL CAPS IMPORTANT!

Please please *please* just read it and don't slam your laptop shut and shout, "There's a crazy Ruth stalking me online!"

I'm not stalking you. And the pics are proof that I'm not crazy. Although it might be hard to tell I'm not crazy from that first one. Don't be afraid! That stain on my shirt is just ketchup. (My BFF, Jedgar Johnston, and I were making our first-ever animated horror short, *Zippy the Zombie Squirrel.* You can find it on YouTube. It is both hysterically funny and totes terrifying!)

Anyway, here's the thing. Do you ever use FaceTrace? It's sort of like Google image search, but way fancier. You put a picture of your face into it and SHAZAM!, it swoops through the entire Internet and gives you ALL the other photos of yourself. It isn't perfect or anything. Once it gave me a picture of a baby monkey, but it was a very very very cute one, so I chose not to be insulted. Anyway, Ruby Starling, THAT is how I found all these pics!

1

Look at them!

(Are you looking?)

At first, I couldn't figure it out. I mean, I haven't been to all those places! I haven't worn all those clothes! And I have never ever had lavender hair!

Then I realized it: All of the pics *aren't* me. Some of them are *you*.

Then — as you can imagine — I thought, well, who *are* YOU? And *why* do you have my face? Is it something *ominous* and terrible and bizarre? Did you steal my identity? WHAT?

My heart was beating super hard.

I looked at the pics for a long, long time.

And then, just like that, it was obvious. I figured it out!!!! It wasn't like in movies when the heroine solves the case and then there is a big swell of music, even though I sort of felt like there should be. My eyes were overflowing with tears. Because . . . well . . .

Ruby Starling, WE ARE IDENTICAL TWINS!

It's not something terrible, after all.

It's something amazing!

I'm trying to imagine what you are doing right now: throwing up or showing someone else in disbelief or smacking your forehead or laughing or crying or fainting or squealing with glee or calling the police or even screaming. I didn't know how to react myself! At all! There isn't even anyone at home for me to *tell* right now, except Caleb, my slobbering golden retriever, and he's not as excited about this as he should be. So I decided to do the only thing I could do, which was to write to you RIGHT AWAY. After all, who is going to know how I feel right this second more than you? Because you must feel *exactly* the same way that I do.

Which is confused! And also, ecstatic!

I have *so* many questions for you, Ruby Starling. They are getting jumbled up inside my fingers even as I try to type them out. Such as, did you KNOW that they *split us up*? Did you know we were adopted out to different families? Did you have ANY IDEA that I existed? And, if so, why didn't I know about *you*? And if you *didn't* know about me, did you always feel like some part of you was missing? And if you *did* know about me, how did you find out? Did YOUR adoptive parents know? And if you knew, why didn't you WRITE? Or call? And ohmygosh, why didn't *anyone* tell me? It seems like this is the kind of thing that shouldn't be a secret! It shouldn't be ALLOWED to be a secret!

Seriously, this is the craziest thing I can even imagine!

On second thought, I suppose that you could be impersonating me for nefarious reasons. What if you ARE? I'm not actually OK with that, so if *that* is what is going on here, I have to ask you to CEASE AND DESIST!

Or . . .

Wait, is this a joke?

Jedgar? JEDGAR ALLEN JOHNSTON?

Is this something *you* made up? Did you plant the photos and the email address and all the other stuff? Are you filming this? Is it a *project*?

If so, that is a tiny bit brilliant (and I totes would never have thought of it!) but also infuriating, and Jedgar, *if* this is you, I'm never speaking to you again, at least not for a while.

But if this is for real? (And I soooooo hope that it is . . .)

Then WRITE BACK RIGHT AWAY, RUBY STARLING.

Yours super sincerely,

Ruth Quayle

FROM: **Ruth Quayle** iamruthquayle@gmail.com

TO: **Jedgar Allen Johnston** JedgarAllenPoe@yahoo.com

I am very very mad. I am *so* mad that my leg is jumping up and down in an uncontrollable angry twitch, which is obvi what they mean by *hopping mad*. I am writing this because I do not trust myself to talk to you without spitting or crying. I know Dad would tell me, "You will not be punished for your anger, you will be punished *by* your anger" (because coincidentally, that is the quote he texted me this morning, as part of his quest to Buddhify my life), but I do not care what wisdom his Buddhist Page-A-Day calendar would apply to this situation. I AM STILL VERY ANGRY.

First of all, JEDGAR, there is a big distance between "funny" and "not funny." It's the length of the Amazon River, plus the Mississippi, the Danube, the Thames, *and* the Tigris and Euphrates, plus whatever other rivers you can name from last semester's geography test, all added together. Do you know how serious this is? It is the *most* serious. You shouldn't be allowed to toy with a person's emotional stuff. It's mean. So if you *are* impersonating my twin sister living in England *and* Photoshopping pics to look like prettier, better-dressed versions of me *and* planting them on a fake British fashion blog and a fake British school website *and* creating fake email addresses to trick me, then it is OVER BETWEEN US. By which I mean "our friendship," not any of that crazy stuff about kissing that you were talking about last Tuesday.

By the way, you don't *actually like*-like me! Your brain is just tricking you into thinking you *like*-like me because I am always around. After you said what you said, I Googled "love." You know, to see what it's all about. And what I found out is that *proximity* is the number-one cause of all love-falling-into feelings! True fact! (It was on Wikipedia.) So it's all just a lie. (Not that you are lying to me! Not that. But rather, your *feelings* are lying to *you*.)

Well, that was a huge relief. So now you know! It was

nothing! Just a mistake! And we can get back to normal, ASAP.

Anyway, if it's *not* you, playing a complicated (but totes impressive!) prank, then guess what? You aren't going to *believe* this, but I have the most amazing, incredible news!

I HAVE FOUND AN IDENTICAL TWIN SISTER LIVING IN GREAT BRITAIN! Specifically, one Ms. Ruby Starling, age 12⅔, who resides in a charming hamlet (possibly) to the north (or south) of (or probably near to) London (I haven't Google Mapped it yet), which is (likely) very picturesque and (maybe) has rolling hills and maybe even sheep or rock stars. Or, if not, then the opposite, such as the totally industrial, filthy, and sadlike town in *Billy Elliot*! Anyway, J., I'm not actually sure where she lives, but *that* doesn't matter.

What does matter is that I have a TWIN! Exclamation point! Bold font! ITALICS!

You know how I'm always saying things like, "I feel like I'm missing something!" and you're like, "Stop being weirder than necessary, Ruth." Well, yes, sure, *you* might think that I feel weird because I was adopted and/or because of Ashley Mary Jane, but now there is a real answer. A better answer!

The answer is: *Ruby Starling.*

Oh, JEDGAR! I feel like I'm going to go completely crazy! Obviously, I wrote her an email RIGHT AWAY, and

I've been running up and down the stairs ever since waiting for her to answer while Caleb barks at me in lazy disgust.

I can't even explain how weird this whole situation is! Writing an email to my *twin sister*! Having a twin sister! It may be the weirdest thing that has ever happened to me, and, as you know, lots of weird things have happened to me.

How long do you think it will take her to write me back? It is 6:00 p.m. in England, where she *lives* (my own twin sister! Living in England! Just there! Existing!), so it's not like she already went to bed and won't answer until morning, amirite? I would answer RIGHT AWAY, wouldn't you? If someone who looked exactly like you sent you an email from halfway around the world?

Jedgar Allen Johnston, if this is a joke you have manufactured as some kind of experimental film project, tell me RIGHT NOW. Right now. Or I swear, Jedgar, I swear, I WILL DO SOMETHING TERRIBLE.

If not . . .

OMG.

Whoa. That's amazing. I mean, like, *if* it's real. And NO! I didn't do that. I didn't do anything. I don't even know how you would do something like that. Would I have to hack your computer? Because I don't know how. I might watch YouTube and edit movies but I would never figure out how to "hack" things just to play mean jokes on my friends. Do you even *know* me? I'd never do that.

Anyway, don't get all mad, but it does sound kind of crazy. I guess you technically *could* have a twin, being adopted and everything, but there are lots of possible reasons why you look so much like that other girl. You could have plenty of relatives you don't know about, doofus. I mean, I look almost exactly like my cousin The Ham, except I'm smaller and less porcine and three years younger. Gene pools can be completely weird. Maybe she is the kid of your third cousin's aunt, and she just happens to have gotten the same combo of proteins that make you look like you. Genes ARE just proteins, you know. Like cheese. Or bacon. (Mmmm, bacon.) You know what I just read? That most girls grow up to look like their father's mother! So maybe you and she both have the same grandmother on your dad's side. Which could make her your half sister. Or your cousin. Think about it.

So, look. I don't want to talk about Tuesday at the park and what I said and what you said. Just so you know, I was *kidding*. I didn't mean it. I mean, I *did* mean it, but just only for that exact moment that I said it. I like you a lot less now, if that makes you feel better.

Have you thought about writing the script for *SHORCA!*? I think a Claymation movie about a shark/orca hybrid chomping its way down the coast is completely genius. It might be the best idea we've ever had! Zombies are like vampires: totally *over*. Which is why *Zippy* got two thumbs down on KidzMakeMovies.com. (Also, because I think my brothers posted at least half the reviews.) Sharks are definitely the next big thing. *SHORCA!* might make us famous on the site or even at Cortez, if Mr. M. lets us show it in art class, like he did with *The Way the Vampires Died*.

Want to come over and work on it? My mom bought us some black and some white clay to make the SHORCAs. There's kind of nothing else you can do about Ruby-Starling-Who-Lives-In-England-And-Looks-Like-You, anyway. I looked at the pictures again and the resemblance is creepy. It'll be cool to see what she says when she writes back.

If she does, I guess.

So there you are,
you: Ruth.
Ruth, alone.
At home.
On the blue couch in the den
that smells like Dad's socks
and Caleb's drooly toys,
thinking about
shark/whale
hybrids chomping their
way across the screen.
The TV is on and you are
eating a cookie (three)
and looking at pictures of you
on the Internet
just to see
how you have changed, since you
last noticed yourself.

And then you find yourself,
there. Look!
Except you aren't you.
You are a different you
existing differently

in England, with funny
English things,
like tea and crumpets
and accents
and fashion sense.
What do you do with that?
You have to suppose
that some people
already know
(like your Real mom, for example)
(and your Real dad)
(except your real parents
are more real than
the Real imagined ones
who ski in the winter
and summer on the Cape
where the sand is kept white and perfect
by hired helpers
because they are probably quite famous,
rich, and misunderstood
and deserve only the best of snow
and beaches)
and aren't telling you,
all of which makes your
heart — Ashley Mary Jane's
heart — beat so
hard that it is like thunder

and the secret is going to be

lightning, flashing down

and leaving a pattern

tattooed on everyone

it touches, if it doesn't

ruin them,

everything,

me, us.

FROM: **Ruth Quayle** iamruthquayle@gmail.com

TO: **Jedgar Allen Johnston** JedgarAllenPoe@yahoo.com

The more I think about it, the more I realize that while it is all totes exciting and everything — having a TWIN! In a different COUNTRY! — it also could mean a lot of serious things! Like, if she IS my twin, then maybe she knows who my parents really are! Or maybe there are more of us! Or who knows what? I mean, at first I was excited, but I thought about it *too* much, and I kind of got freaked out.

I can't come over right now! Dad's here. He came home early because Mom is away, as you know, being smart and important in Boston, and so I had no one to call except for him, of course, when this momentous thing happened! He didn't answer, being ALSO busy and important, but I left him a message that just said, "I NEED YOU! DAD!" (I may have been having a panic attack at the time! I couldn't really breathe right!) and so he raced home, thinking I was trapped under something heavy, such as the dinosaur in the dining room. He burst in the door shouting, "WAS THERE AN EARTHQUAKE? ARE YOU OK?"

To be honest, he seemed a little disappointed that there was no earthquake and I was like, "Dad, I am fine." I was, at the time, calmly lying on the couch, sweating, with nothing heavier on me than Caleb, who was actually pinning me down to stop me from running up and down the stairs anymore. (It makes him nervous when people exercise inside.)

I could tell that Dad was completely confused about why he had to abandon his paperwork (which he hates anyway! so really I did him a favor!) to race home when I was A-OK, and he wasn't sure how to decode the mystery that is me, Ruth Quayle. I should have just told him, but now that he was actually home, I was scared to talk about Ruby Starling. What if he got mad? What if he got sad? What if he had no idea what I was talking about? What if he laughed? I mean, I know he *wouldn't*, because he's Dad and he's mostly awesome, but lately he's been laughing at lots of stuff I say, even when I don't mean it to be funny. So instead of telling the truth, I told him that I thought I saw a burglar climbing in through the skylight next door, but it turned out to be a false alarm, just their overly large cat, Arthur, enjoying an afternoon nap in the sun.

I think he knows something is up, though, because he keeps asking me if I'm OK in his overly concerned Dad-voice. Maybe he is noticing that my leg won't stay still. But he's not asking the right questions! And I *can't* just blurt it out! It sounds too . . . weird. Besides, the shock might be too much for him. Or for *me*. I'm the one with the heart thing, after all.

Dad's solution to everything is either to a) read about Buddhism and/or meditate or b) for us to do something together. I'm just not in the mood for Buddha and/or sitting still, so he called in to his office to say that I'm sick, and he's playing *Doctor You* on the Xbox. This is a "together" thing in that I watch and he plays. It's never my turn because he's so good at it, which is grossly unfair. He did a *jillion* years in medical school, so it would be totes embarrassing if he couldn't take the appendix out of an animated elderly man, wouldn't it? On the plus side, seeing as I never get a chance to even try, I can just hit Send/Receive on my in-box to see if Ruby Starling's answer has arrived, and *completely freak out* while pretending to be relaxing all la-di-da and joyful on the couch, applauding Dad's amazeballs surgical techniques.

I can't believe Ruby Starling *still* hasn't replied. What's wrong with her? How can she not be falling all over herself to answer RIGHT AWAY? Maybe the Internet is broken in England. I'm going to write to her again using a different email address that I found right there on her school's website. (It says that all the students' email addresses are their firstnamelastname@schoolname.co.uk. Why would this be public? That's crazy!) (Also, I Google Mapped her school, and doesn't it look amazing? It looks like something from an antique novel about English boarding schools featuring girls named Gwendoline and Beatrix!) After I did that, I did a Google Maps walking tour of the town where she lives and it's the prettiest town ever! Just exactly what I'd pictured something British to be! With old stone buildings and rolling green hills and country lanes! I didn't picture the Starbucks or the McDonald's, but I guess those are everywhere, which, frankly, I think is an appalling affront to picturesque English villages. You can practically HEAR the clip-clop of history galloping down the cobbled streets! Nothing here is anywhere nearly as interesting-looking, I can tell you that.

Ruby is so LUCKY.

Also, when it comes to that thing you don't want to talk about, I *knew* you were kidding but also not kidding. I hadn't given one thought to *kissing* until you brought it up, and then all I could think about was slugs and how they leave that silvery trail of slime all over the place that absolutely cannot be washed off. And I have to be honest, when I thought of the slugs, I gagged just a little bit.

I talked *that* whole thing over with Mom and Dad at Pizza Prima Heaven, where we went for dinner that night, and they agreed that I would know when I was ready to want to even think about kissing another person, and that time would be when I didn't also think about things that make me barf. It's not *you*, Jedgar! I'm just 150% not ready! They also said that they knew this was coming because we are that age, and I should get more friends besides you, and I told them they were ridiculous because I have plenty of friends, even though I don't really. I AM practically almost friends with Tink Aaron-Martin, who is mostly cool and funny and not evil and practicing to be too beautiful to exist, as though prettiness is a full-time job. Why is every other girl at our school so awful? I mean, Freddie Blue Anderson? Stella Wilson-Rawley? I can't even imagine being friends with those girls. Or, worse, BEING those girls.

Weirdly enough, Freddie Blue Anderson happened to ALSO be in Pizza Prima Heaven at the time, having dinner with her dad, who was texting up a storm while ignoring her completely. Mom was all, "YOU SHOULD GO SAY HI TO THAT POOR GIRL! ISN'T SHE IN YOUR CLASS AT CORTEZ?" And I was all, "I WOULD RATHER LIGHT MYSELF ON FIRE AND LEAP INTO A TAR PIT, THANK YOU VERY MUCH!" As awesome as Mom is, sometimes she just does NOT get it. Then she said, "It's just that boy-girl friendships are fraught with drama. It would be great if you had more female friends. Female friends are SO important in life!" Which is rich, because I'm pretty sure that all Mom's friends are male, at least all the dinosaur scientist types that she works with, and Dad and basically everyone else we know is a man.

Anyway, I don't think I have ever heard anyone use the word "fraught" in a sentence about *me* before. And I thought you would find it interesting, because you like words so much, and so I said, "Jedgar would love that word! 'Fraught'!" My mom started laughing and Dad threw an ice cube at her, and the waiter told us to settle down because Dad actually missed and the ice cube landed on the pizza of an elderly woman in the next booth. I got the hiccups from laughing so hard, and FBA kept shooting eye-rolling glances at me across the room while she nibbled on a piece of lettuce. (Who eats lettuce in a pizza restaurant?)

Then we started talking about dinosaur cloning.

We are ALWAYS talking about dinosaur cloning.

Which is OK, because it's better than talking about how I've never had a girl as a good friend before, because when we talk about that, it makes me feel weird, like I forgot to do something important and I'll never be able to catch up. It's too late. That ship has sailed. And I will be bereft and alone forever.

Nothing personal! You are a terrific BFF and I don't need any girl friends anyway, so whatever! Pretend I didn't mention it!

And seriously, I do not want to talk about it anymore either, so let's just let it go. Forever. (By "it," I don't mean "our lifelong friendship," I just mean the *thing* that you said that may or may not have made our friendship *fraught*.)

I will write some ideas for *SHORCA!* right now because it is never going to be my turn in this game.

SHORCA!:

The TRUE and TERRIFYING Tale of the Shark/Orca That Ate Everyone on the Coast of Oregon and Some People on Washington and California Beaches, Also

Written by Ruth Quayle and Animated by Jedgar Johnston

Scene One, Act One

Show GIRL and BOY racing down the hill to the beach on a hot sunny day to sound track of hipster music, such as ukulele. BOY slips on a slug and scrapes his knee. [See what I did there? Slugs are dangerous! And should be avoided!] Show the fall in slow-mo to swelling music! Horns and cymbals!

BOY: I'm bleeding!
GIRL: It's nothing! Let's go swimming!

BOY: It's not like sharks will smell blood and devour me! There are no sharks here.

GIRL (*in foreshadowy voice*): Well, not that you know of! Besides, everyone knows that salt water is a terrific antiseptic!

[*BOY and GIRL get to beach and run into the water, again in slow-mo.*]

GIRL: (*screams*)
BOY: (*screams*)
GIRL: (*screams more*)
BOY: (*screams more*)
(*Etc!*)

SHORCA chomps up BOY and GIRL and then burps underwater — show burp bubbles rising to the music. Red swirls of blood in the water! Terrifying, etc!

JEDWIN and ROXANNE, best friends, are watching from the shore.

JEDWIN: Something very scary and mysterious is going on here! And I, Jedwin, and you, Roxanne, will get to the bottom of it if it's the last thing we do! [*Shakes fist at the heavens.*]

ROXANNE: We are an amazing team, even though we aren't boyfriend-girlfriend and never will be!

They give a teamwork fist bump and/or elaborate handshake.

What do you think? That's probably not up to my usual level of awesome writerliness, I know. I'm having too much internal turmoil to make it sound any good. The dialogue in *Zippy* was soooo stellar. I can't believe we only got a B from Mr. M. He usually loves our stuff.

Oh, it's my turn for the Xbox! Gadzooks. Dad must have been distracted. Maybe there was an earthquake.

SEND RECEIVE SEND RECEIVE SEND RECEIVE! WHY WON'T SHE ANSWER?

FROM: **Ruby Starling** starling_girl@mail.com

TO: **Fiona** fififionafifi@aol.co.uk;
Chlophie!!! chlophie@hotmail.co.uk

Please read this e I've just got from someone called 'Ruth', from a gmail account. She sounds American. She — if it is a 'she' — sent it twice, to my reg mail *and* my school one. Do you think someone's stalking me on the Internet?

I knew submitting those photos to FashionForwardIsta
.co.uk was the worst idea, Fi. Mum would have seriously had
a wobbler if she'd seen them. I thought you deleted them
when your dad discovered it! Remember how he gave us
that lecture about how the entire Internet is basically where
bad guys go to find girls to kidnap? This is worse than either
Mum or your dad finding out. And suppose your dad is
right, after all? And some madman has found my photos and
made up a story of us being twins separated at birth to lure
me into a false sense of security so he can strike when I'm
not expecting it? Because I'd *know* if I had a twin. So this
must be something scary and strange. It has to be!

I mean, I am not taking it seriously. Except just a little
bit. What kind of name is 'Jedgar'? It's a made-up name,
right? I bet he just stole that from Jedward so that I'd be
blinded by popstar fandom and not read too much into the
details. Well, HA. I don't even like Jedward! And I've never
even met a Ruth who isn't 82 years old and a friend of Nan's.
You'd think if you were going to make up a story, you'd at
least make it seem like it was real.

I'm obviously not even adopted, so why would she/he
think I'd believe this daft story in the first place? Although
if you look at the pictures, she *does* look an awful lot like
me. What would *you* do if someone sent you pictures of
yourself that aren't you?

What do you all think? Is it a prank or should I be scared?

Ruby, you are being stalked!!!!!!! It is *definitely* stalker behaviour. Don't you remember that film they showed us at school last term about things to be wary of, things about strange men? This is *just* like that!

He's obvs got your info from the school website, where there is that shot of you winning the spelling trophy in Year 4, and now he's *obsessed* with you. That must be it. It's quite a good photo. You look all sparkly in it. (Not that you don't always look good, 'course you do.) (That sad fashion blog only got about a hundred hits a day! And most of them were me, checking to see if anyone had given you five stars for your fashion. Why would a stalker look at a fashion-of-the-day site, for goodness' sake? This isn't my fault! Can't be!)

What I think is that this 'Ruth' is trying to weaken your defences. These creeps always say 'Oh, I've lost my dog, help me find it, little girl!' and then they lure you into their unmarked white van with no windows and then . . . it's all over.

I showed the note to my dad, and he said, 'Ooooooh, boy, what's that all about then?', and you just know that means he thinks it's trouble, like he was getting a copper's sort of sense, like he does. But then he said, 'Spam email's getting awfully sophisticated, maybe it's an advert? Or that phishing, like?' But what does he know? He's only just a constable. He never even did his A-levels. I think it's much more likely to be a stalker who is also a Photoshopping genius who has gone mad with cutting and pasting you into scenes from some American girl's life!

Ruby, I'm scared for you now! You'll have to be really cautious. Not that I think you should panic. Don't *panic*. But don't help anyone find a puppy either.

Fi

Gosh, Ruby, this is so exciting! What if you actually do have a twin in America? That's fab! We *lurrrrrve* America. Everyone is so good-looking and posh there, with their white teeth and huge cars and things. And their really, really excellent snack foods. It's so much better than boring old stodgy dull England. If you move there, can we visit? Specially if you live somewhere amazeog, like LA or New York! Pretty please?

We're jooooking! We think it's just a prank, probs. It's like someone's trying to get to you 'cause he fancies you, like that spotty boy from the chip shop on Dagen's Road. They have medicine for spots like his now, so one day he will have lovely glowing skin and maybe even decent teeth, and you'll say, 'Oh, why was I so awful to him when he's such a dreamboat now?' If you look quite closely at him, you can see he's mostly symmetrical, and *That's Teen!* mag says that symmetry is *basically* the same thing as beauty. So he's actually OK, yeah.

HOOOOoooooiiiii.

Oh, that was Chloe, she says hi. She's laughing too hard to type properly. CHLOE, STOP IT.

She says you should tell this 'Ruth' (or the Chip Shop Boy) to get stuffed. I think so too. But I'd never say that because manners are terrifically important to . . .

Oh, OK. OK CHLOE. STOP.

So, what we think is just that you should say, 'PLEASE get stuffed'.

Bisou! Bisou! (That means 'kiss kiss' in French. *Très sophisticate!*)

Sophie & Chloe

Dear Nan,

Something strange is happening. I got a message in my email today. It's a very bizarre message, Nan. (Yes, I *know* you never trusted email. And I know that opening actual letters is lovely! But people just don't do that now. The post's too slow, isn't it? By the time it gets delivered, it's already old news!)

But THIS is a real letter that I'm writing to you! The sort you like. I hope this letter makes you happy wherever you are, because it must be somewhere, even if I think the whole idea of heaven being a big, happy field full of friendly dead relatives is mad. (That wouldn't be 'heaven', it would be pretty dreadful. Imagine having to make small talk with horrid Uncle Charlie for the rest of time?)

This email that I'm talking about is from someone named Ruth. And — you'll probably have a laugh at this — this 'Ruth' says that she's my twin sister, living in America!

When I read that bit, though, I had this strange feeling that I was falling down, even though I was sitting on the floor. (I was in my bedroom wardrobe — you know how I've always loved small cosy spaces, and it's practically a little room, like Harry Potter's cupboard under the stairs! Except nicer — I'm leaning on the cushion you made with the rabbit on it. The rabbit is almost completely worn off now. The sad little worn-out rabbit makes me extra sad. I just so wish you were here to fix it.)

There were all these pics attached to the email, Nan. Pictures of me, Ruby Elizabeth Starling. Only some of them weren't of me at all, but someone who looks just *exactly* like a slightly smaller, crookeder, scribblier version of me. The girls say that the whole thing is probably the work of a stalker (or else the Chip Shop Boy with the spotty face!) and a good bit of Photoshopping, but I don't know. How would that make sense? Anyway, I have one of those bad feelings that buzz round inside my brain, scaring me, and I feel like I have to stay in here and hang on tight to something, just in case.

Remember when you died? Well, obviously you do. Shouldn't think you'd forget *that*. But right before you went, you started breathing strangely, rasping and whistling and groaning and then stopping and then suddenly starting back up. My whole life feels like that right now, all stops and starts and scary sounds. I'm scared, even though 'scared' seems like the wrong thing to feel. A normal person would have a laugh and then move on. Not me! I think it's *something*. And I'm really dreadfully afraid, and my heart is doing that twirling-around beat and my hands are sweating, like I'm on the edge of a cliff, about to jump, like I can't stop myself from bending my knees and taking off into the nothing.

Not that I'd ever do that, Nan! Don't worry.

I know you're saying, 'Well, darling girl, not everyone is a villain, you know'. But NAN, I can't possibly have a twin I don't know about! That only happens on telly or in the tabloids. I wish

I had a proper family so I could show my parents and ask them what to do. But I *can't* show this email to Mum. She's only barely keeping it together since you left us, and if I mentioned this, she'd fall apart, like she did when that Dermott with the gold front tooth ditched her at the village Christmas party. Do you remember that? That was before you first got ill, before we heard about the cancer and everything turned sour. You took me shopping in London so Mum could get herself together, and I bought those fab blue suede boots. I love those. I still look at them all the time when I'm sad. The way they smell and the way the suede feels and the way, when you rub it, it changes colour. Those are the nicest boots I've ever had, new and everything, not from the Thrift. I wish I could have stopped my feet from growing.

Anyway, 'Ruth' is obviously bonkers (or fake), because I'm not adopted, which I'd have to have been for her story to make sense. It's not like I even could be and don't know it, because we look exactly alike, me and Mum! (And you!) And there's that photo in the corridor of Mum with her big stomach when she was preggers with me. She was huge! That can't be made up.

I wish you could write back, but I suppose you can't. How could you get a letter to me? How many stamps does it take to get a letter from heaven? And how can someone be allowed to just email me from who-knows-where and interrupt my already-disastrous life with a bunch of photos that turn me upside down? Why can cancer just swoop through and take the best people? Why can't all mums be really really really good at being mums, not just at, say, art? Nan, if I thought Mum would know what to do, I'd ask her, but I just don't think she'd know, would she? Why is everything so unfair, basically ALL the time?

I have loads of other questions too. Those are just for starters!

Well, YOU can't answer any of them, can you? Unless . . . Well, if you can, please please please do.

Hang on, Nan. There was just a huge crash in Mum's old studio! She's not here, she's at the new studio she's renting above the gastropub, because it's close to the library, which is where her new installation is going. Plus, she says she can't stand to be in the old studio without you there wandering about, telling her that her latest work looks like rubbish. 'But beautiful rubbish, darling', you'd always say. 'The best possible rubbish. I'm sure it'll be lovely when it's done'.

Nan, was that you? Crashing? Are you trying to tell me something? Now I'm even more panicky. I'm having a hard time catching my breath! Should I call 999? I don't even believe in ghosts!

Love,
Ruby

Mum, can you pick up some paracetamol on your way home? I have a bit of a headache. It's *nothing.* Don't worry about it, if you can't, if you're busy. I understand. Maybe I'll see you later, but maybe I'll turn in early. Actually, never mind, Mum. I'm fine now.

Hi darling, sorry, in an awful rush, heading into a meeting with the committee for final approval of this . . . but yes, I'll try to remember. If I don't, just pinch that bit between your thumb and your finger quite hard. Then count to ten or twenty. Oh, now I've got clay all over this iPhone! Bother.
xooxxxoo Delilah

Sorry, darling, awfully distracted. Obviously I meant to sign off as 'Mummy', not as 'Delilah'! But you knew who it was! Of course. Sorry, sorry. Back to work! I'll rush home as soon as I can. Maybe put a cold cloth on your head, you know how that helps. Feel better!

XXOO

Hi guys!
I am writing you this note to say "I love you." I think you are totes amazeballs as parents, even though you are probably looking at your screens with raised eyebrows, thinking, "I'll translate those words later using online slang dictionaries!" (Spoiler: "Totes amazeballs" means "you are great"!)

I just wanted to say that.

I think maybe something MOMENTOUS, like really really big, will happen soon in all of our lives, and you might be . . . *something* about it. Like mad or sad or happy. Or *I* might be mad or sad or happy! Or something else! And before it all goes down, I felt like sending you this note from the couch, even though Dad is only ten feet away from me! (Hi Dad!) No, don't worry, I am not suicidal or running away with a boy I met in a Minecraft chat room, swearsies. I'm kind of over Minecraft anyway. It gets boring after a while, and I don't like video games when I could be making movies with Jedgar or skateboarding at the park or reading poetry or writing it or practicing ancient yoga techniques such as headstands or . . . doing anything else.

I just ALSO wanted to say that you're doing an OK job of raising me and overall things are basically pretty good around here! (A bigger allowance wouldn't hurt. OR a pony.) So remember that, OK? If stuff gets weird.

If you're looking for me, Dad, I'm taking Caleb for a walk because I'm tired of watching you playing the Xbox. I'm practically getting carsick from staring at the screen while your on-screen hands swish around. You should probably step away from the TV. It's bad for your eyes or your brain or both.

And before you ask: Yes, I know it is hot. Yes, I will take water. Yes, I will be home for dinner. Yes, I will keep Caleb on the leash so he doesn't run away again and show up three days later having eaten all of Mrs. Martin's compost. Yes, my phone is in my pocket, just in case. Yes, yes, yes.

Have a good trip, Mom! Miss you already!

xo

Ruth

FROM: **Gen Quayle** Gen@usdinolab.org

TO: **Ruth Quayle** iamruthquayle@gmail.com

Hi Sweetie,

What on earth is going on? Can you call me? I'm stuck at the airport in Boston waiting for a rental car. They want to give me a van. Can you imagine? I'll look like a soccer mom! Ugh. Worst. I've explained that you don't play soccer because you aren't that kind of a kid AND I'm traveling alone AND lecturing at Harvard, but they don't seem to care. Some people are completely unimpressed by science. Or maybe I need a better hairstyle.

Call me! I'll keep the phone on. You are worrying me!

Lots of love,

Mommy

P.S. Unplug the Xbox! Your dad has a serious problem with that game.

Love you, too! Glad you remembered water. Phew, this heat is something else. Hope it doesn't trigger one of your headaches. The news this morning when I was driving in said that temps would top 110! And people think global warming isn't a thing. Fools. Those people are going to be the first to perish when we heat the earth up so much, life can't be sustained. Actually, I guess in that scenario, attitude won't count. (But it usually does!)

Anyway, remember what we have learned so far from The Great Buddhism Project: Life is suffering. I know that sounds depressing, but I'm sure that when we are finished working our way through this calendar, you will understand that it's not a bad thing. I find that it just makes sense. For now, check out this quote: "When you realize how perfect everything is, you will tilt your head back and laugh at the sky." Ah, that's one of my favorites, for sure.

I have to go back up to the hospital for rounds after I'm done with this level. Wait for me before you eat, then we can watch TV together and have an entirely unhealthy feast. (Corn dogs?) Don't tell Mom. And please don't tell her that I played this game for three straight hours. Or else.

Dad

I've just come from Chloe's. She and Soph have made up a whole thing where you've been kidnapped by a stalker and taken somewhere awful, like Salford or worse, and we have to take the train up and rescue you, like amazeog super-heroes. (Oh, we aren't to say 'fab' anymore. It's now AMAZEOG, OK?) I told them they were being ridic, because you are much too sensible to be kidnapped — well, *obviously* — so you won't need rescuing. You may be the youngest of us, but you're by far the cleverest, and if anyone is going to rescue anyone, it will be you rescuing us, I should think.

Did you e the stalker and tell him off? I was reading a true crime book of Dad's last night where the story was almost exactly the same. Except it wasn't a strange email sent from someone claiming to be a twin, it was an actual letter. And it took place in the 1970s in Hampshire. Still, it was *really* upsetting.

I'm scared for you. You need to protect yourself, Ruby! Be the offence, not the defence, like we learned from Creepy Coach Cratchett. She's right! Field hockey rules do apply to life a *lot*. I never believed her until just now.

I'm replying to the e now! I had one of those panic attacks again. I didn't want to tell Mum, but I wanted her to come home, so I told her I had a headache. 'Course, she *can't* come home. I was just being silly. I know she's really busy sculpting me so that I can sit reading a book in front of the library forever and ever. I wish she'd let me pick the book. I love Harry Potter! I just don't know that I'll want to read it for all of eternity, like I will be once she's done.

It's probably karma that now I do have quite a bad migraine. Or maybe I've got psychic powers and I knew I was going to get one! You'd think I could use powers like that to get Nate to love me back properly or even just to win the Lotto or something.

Am not sure what to say to 'Ruth', not really, so am just going to start typing and see what happens. Fi, I've been thinking, what if it's real? I mean, I *know* it's not. 'Course it's not. But what if it — she — is? What if I *do* have a twin?

Oh, Roobs, I'm sorry. It *is* upsetting, but don't get worked up. The panicky things are just because of all the stress of your nan dying. The Mole used to get those when he was a kid, and he had a therapist who made him tap his legs and chant, 'I tap the power within me to make the panic attack stop'! It was awfully embarrassing. (For me, I mean. He seemed to like it.) Anyway, I think you're still not OK yet after everything. You just have to give yourself a bit of time. I forget sometimes that you're only 12. You're so mature, like me.

That e is *not* real. It's just some mad old yobbo who is trying to frighten you. You're doing the right thing. Write me back when you hear anything. If you do. Which you won't, because your note will scare him off. Those types are always frightened off by people who are tough and fight back, that's what my dad says. Be *really* firm in your note. Oh, Dad also says you should take a self-defence class. They're offering it at Mick's on Tuesdays at 7. Ask your mum. The Mole is going, as though he'll ever need to defend himself from anyone, as he never leaves the cave in the basement that he calls a bedroom, and if he does, the stench of his feet will keep all bad guys at bay.

FROM: **Ruby Starling** starling_girl@mail.com

TO: **Ruth Quayle** iamruthquayle@gmail.com

'Ruth':
You are mad. Bonkers.

Get stuffed.

And don't write to me again, please. Your note was very upsetting.

Yours truly,

Ruby Starling

PS — You are very good at Photoshop. A little TOO good, don't you think?

FROM: **Ruby Starling** starling_girl@mail.com

TO: **Fiona** fififionafifi@aol.co.uk;
Chlophie!!! chlophie@hotmail.co.uk

There, now I've written to her/him (see attached). Is not clever or anything, but I wanted it to be short, like a slap. I feel like I *should* tell someone, but I'm not going to, because if Mum got wind of it, she'd be away with the fairies. She's already got enough on with that library project. It's a *brilliant* statue, isn't it? I don't know how she can sculpt people who look so real. When you see her art, it's hard to imagine she's the same person who can't boil up some carrots without setting the stove on fire and melting the pot.

I just . . . I do sometimes wish she'd sculpt people who weren't *me*. Or that she wasn't so good at it. She's better at figuring out pretend versions of me than she is at figuring out the real me! Not that there is anything to figure out, but what if there were? Worse, everyone is going to know it's meant to be me — that statue, that is. And Hawkster and his mates will graffiti something rude on it, and Mum will be crushed. Why are boys such wazzocks?

That Spotty Chip Shop Boy is the worst of the lot. You mustn't ever mention my name and his together again. (Not that we actually know his name.) Nan would have said that you're just inviting fate to come and have a cuppa, saying things like that. And my fate is NOT the Spotty Chip Shop Boy. I am in love with Nate from STOP and no one else. Not ever. Don't roll your eyes. It's real love, girls. Truly. Nate's freckles and upright hair are so . . . *phwoar*. Regular boys are *so* dull and always look like they have food in their teeth and smelly breath. And they don't understand *fashion*, not like me and Nate do. I can hardly wait to be 18. Then Nate and I will meet for real, and you'll all stop having a laugh whenever I mention his name.

Good job, you! I knew you'd handle it brilliantly, and you did. Shouldn't think you'd hear from him again, the creep.

It's not that I don't believe that Nate could love you, it's more that he looks like a piglet. Why should you love him? He could store marbles in those huge nostrils! Besides, I saw some pics of him on the Internet with that prat, Sig McCallum. Nate's looking *insufferable* with his smirk and square jaw. He'll soon be robbing newsagents or having tantrums on Twitter. Everyone thinks so. Why can't you fall in love with someone nicer, like Bill Ex? Drummers are much more swoony and don't have the massive ego problems of lead singers. Even Dad says that Ringo was the nicest Beatle.

And don't fool yourself, Nate has people to tell him what to wear! In real life, he probably dresses like a chav in too-small T-shirts and tracksuit bottoms. I think you should start your *own* fashion empire when you're done with school and never mind Nate, who will be washed up by then. I'll be your assistant and we'll both be impossibly glam and admired the world over! Or at least in northern England and maybe the more fashionable parts of Wales.

Your mum's sculpture *is* brill. You're *lucky* your mum is so cool and weird and *different*. My parents are so boring.

Living here with them is like living inside an actual yawn, all grey and mingy. That's why I read so much. You don't have to, because you've always got so much on!

Dad says to tell you if anyone wrecks your mum's latest, he will take care of it. I'm not sure what that means but he says to tell you anyway.

FROM: **Chlophie!!!** chlophie@hotmail.co.uk

TO: **Ruby Starling** starling_girl@mail.com

We were just having a bit of fun about the spotty boy. We knoooooow your heart belongs to Nate. Nate the Great! True love! Etcetera and so on!

Glad you got rid of the creepster! What a weirdo. 'Get stuffed' was the best bit. Well, was really the only bit, if you think about it. Was quite a short note. But good! We're applauding! Standing up and everything!

Are you going to Hawkster's do on Friday night? He's sometimes not half bad, even though he's mostly awful. His lovely eyes are all dark and mysterious and piratey. And he's so completely funny! Sometimes his jokes just leave us inside out, howling with laughter.

Oh, Ru-Ru, we need to borrow some clobber. Something glam that makes us look taller and more posh, like fashion models, yeah? Soph says that she bets the party ends up with all of us just watching football or worse, *talking*, but she hasn't got a clue, most of the time. I keep trying to tell her, it could be worse. We could be staying home watching telly and waiting for our lives to begin. At least a party is SOMETHING, even if it's dreadful.

SOPH, I was just teasing, not for real. You know I think you're brill!

Anyway, Ru, just in case it's a real bash, we need to be prepared to look amazeog. So it's OK then, the sparkly tops? You're a star! Thanks!

FROM: **Ruby Starling**   starling_girl@mail.com

TO: **Chlophie!!!**   chlophie@hotmail.co.uk

You can wear some of my things but GIVE THEM BACK PROPERLY CLEAN! I know that *secretly* you're both trying to impress the Spotty Chip Shop Boy by looking modelly and glam. Probably he will fall forever in lurve with you because of your fab style, and you will each one day have 18 of his spotty babies and call them all 'Chip' and I will send them posh gifts from Paris where Nate and I have our summer flat.

No, I am NOT going to Hawkster's. Never! He's the

worst of all of them at our school. If there was a Biggest Wazzock trophy, he'd win it. And he's plug ugly, to boot.

PS — I don't think 'amazeog' is an actual word.

FROM: **Ruth Quayle** iamruthquayle@gmail.com

TO: **Ruby Starling** starling_girl@mail.com

Dear Ruby Starling,

I am not a stalker! I am Ruth Elizabeth Quayle, age 12⅔. I was born on October 30 at Lenox Hill Hospital in NYC. Sounds familiar, amirite? (But if I'm wrong, tell me now! I just know that I'm not. I'm not, am I?)

I don't believe in coincidences. My parents always say that a coincidence is just science proving again that things work the way they are supposed to, *predictably*. We are twins. It's science!

As Buddha would say, "Three things cannot be long hidden: the sun, the moon, and the truth." (My dad has decided that I need to learn more about Buddhism, so has bought us a Page-A-Day Buddhist calendar as a "jumping-off point." We are not all the way through it yet, obviously, as it is not December, but I already feel better. Highly recommend! I haven't quite got the hang of meditating yet, though. It's much too boring and still.)

Oh, Ruby Starling, can't you see that *this* — us being twins — is the truest true thing?

The weird thing is that when I got your note, I *did* feel like a bad guy for a few minutes. *What am I doing, stalking this poor girl in England?* I thought. *Who am I becoming? A madman?*

Then I remembered that I'm *not* stalking you and I'm *not* a bad guy or even a guy at all. I AM RUTH ELIZABETH QUAYLE, AGE 12⅔. I don't even have Photoshop! And you are my twin. You MUST be. Just LOOK at the pics.

Then I started to think about being twins. A lot. And what it means. And Ruby Starling, I have to admit, that it was basically like a crashing and unexpected tidal wave of feelings that I collapsed under. For a few minutes, I had to lie down on the floor beside my bed. I was just totes overwhelmed! The feelings were like water pulling me under!

Then I kind of scooched over until I was actually UNDER my bed. You probably think that's super crazy, but sometimes I feel like there is just too much space around me and I need to get somewhere small and safe. Do you know what I mean? Anyway, that's how I felt. It was extremely dusty under there and I started to sneeze quite a lot and somehow I hit my head on the under-the-bed-support-metal-thingy. Luckily, it didn't bleed. I don't clot very well, but that's a whole other story I'll tell you later. ("Clot" is a terrible word, don't you think? It makes me think of disgusting clumps of sour milk.)

Eventually I came out from under the bed and started Googling. I Google everything. Always. There is lots of amazeballs info out there about all the things! Everything! Anything! I've now intensely studied the Wikipedia entry for twins (and you should too). Because if we are (and we obvi are!) identical twins, for real, then for a little while WE WERE ACTUALLY THE SAME PERSON. Does that totes give you chills? My arms are *popping* with goose bumps, just like the time Jedgar made me go into a haunted house all alone, but with a camera taped to my head. (We were making a fake documentary called *Ghost House*. Do you believe in ghosts? Because I *definitely* do now that I have seen one, for reals. I mean, I didn't actually SEE one, but I sensed that she was there! Which is practically the same thing!)

If we are twins — and we HAVE TO BE — then we have basically all the same cells! Identical DNA and what-not! WE ARE ACTUALLY CLONES! It's just that if they started calling identical twins "clones," then people would think they were being whipped up in test tubes, so I suppose that's why they stick with "twins."

I am trying to put all the pieces together of HOW and WHY and WHAT THE WHAT of our twinning. And I just want to know *everything right away*. I feel like my heart is going to erupt out of my chest and go tearing off down the street on my skateboard. The trouble is that Mom is the one I usually ask all my unusual questions, but she is in

BOSTON. I could call her or Skype her or FaceTime her, but then she'd sense how freaked out I am, and SHE would then probably freak out and come home. Her work is totes the most important thing to her, ever, so I'd feel terrible that I messed it up. She's RIGHT NOW delivering lectures at Harvard University about cloning the lufengosaurus, which we call the Luffster. She's worked really hard for this. The lufengosaurus was (and will be again, if Mom gets her way!) a huge, grass-eating dinosaur the size of a cement mixer. We have a life-size replica of a fossil of a baby one in the dining room. She takes up the entire space where a table and any other regular furniture would normally be, so she lives in exquisite — but tragically lonely! — luxury. We call her Luffetta and she is completely adorbs.

Anyway, some archaeologists found a bunch of lufengosaurus cells in a fossilized dinosaur egg in China. Mom believes she (well, her team) can make a new dinosaur out of it — just like that, she can clone one. It sounds *completely* impossible and slightly crazy to even THINK about. It's totes Jurassic Park! Hollywood! But Mom says it's just *science,* which is all logical, perfectly shaped ideas clicking together to make one big idea that changes everything. (For *some* people, it clicks, that is. However! I am not one of those people. It is super hard having parents who are brilliant and excellent science types, when you have to study for a billion extra hours to just get a B in middle-school science class.)

Anyway, here's what I just realized: If Mom and her team ever *do* get to clone the Luffster, then he or she will be basically a delayed twin with another lufengosaurus who died before he or she was even born. Twins who share the same genes! Like *us*! Weird, amirite? She may even be *Luffetta's* twin! Poor tragic Luffetta.

BUT I CAN'T ASK MOM ABOUT ANY OF THIS BECAUSE SHE WON'T BE BACK FOR THREE DAYS! And what will I even say? How will I tell her that I've found you? What will *she* say? Or think? OR DO?

Oh Ruby. This is too much. Hang on. BRB!

Ruth

FROM: **Ruth Quayle** iamruthquayle@gmail.com

TO: **Ruby Starling** starling_girl@mail.com

OK, I am back (not that you could tell that I was gone!)

I just couldn't stand it. So I did it. I asked my dad about *you*, Ruby Starling.

"Dad," I said formally, while also recording the conversation on my iPod in case I had to refer back to it later (which I am doing). "How is it that I have come to have a twin that I was not aware of?"

"What?" he said. "What on earth are you talking about, Rooty? Want some bumps on a log?" (He was munching on some celery sticks with peanut butter and raisins on top.) (He sometimes calls me Rooty, which is basically the worst, but I let it go because he's my dad and he says that all nicknames mean "I love you." Which, if you think about it, is better than "Ruth," which means "a feeling of pity, distress, or grief.") He looked genuinely perplexed, which means he either DOESN'T know about you, or is a terrific actor! Either way, instead of embracing me and confessing the whole sordid and mysterious truth — whatever it is — he said, "That's . . . ridiculous! I mean, probably."

!

I know, right?

"Probably"?

Then he looked at your pictures on the laptop that I thrust toward him and squinted and then blinked a whole bunch of times in a row like there was an eyelash in his eye. Then he sighed and said that he would know if I had a twin because it was illegal to separate twins during adoptions and had been since, oh, he didn't know, maybe since way back in the 1970s. Maybe. Or at least he thinks he saw that in a movie once, or maybe it was a documentary or a talk show. Or it might have just been something he read in a book.

He paused. And *then* he said, "At least, I *think* so. . . ."

Then his voice trailed off like the drippings of a melting

Häagen-Dazs ice cream bar that was falling off its stick, and he said, "It was a closed adoption . . . ," and he dripped away again. "I mean, we didn't ask about . . ."

Then he said, "Really, that IS strange how *much* you resemble each other. Plus, you look to be the same age. But then again, when you think about all the ways eyes and noses and mouths can be arranged on a face, you're bound to have a double or two. They've even found identical snowflakes, you know. And you have to consider the idea that you found these photographs on the Internet, and you can't trust things you find on the Internet. My patients always think that *blah blah blah etc., etc.*" (Dad's über-favorite topic of conversation is "Mass Hypochondria Created By The Plethora Of Medical Information Available On The Web Today." TRUST ME when I say it is a totes boring paragraph and I have deleted it here for the sake of your sanity.)

Then he laughed in a way that suggested he didn't think anything at all was funny and began staring out the window with an expression of extreme sadness mingled with confusion, sort of like how Caleb looks when he loses his stuffed mouse, Jaunty.

So I said, "Dad? Dad?" and tried to get his attention by waving my hands in his face. I accidentally hit his left eye, but not hard enough to hurt as much as he made out it did. "Dad," I said patiently, "can you call the agency and ask them if I had a twin? Can you threaten to sue them and scare them into telling you? Do anything! Do what you have to do! This is the most important thing that's happened ever in my whole entire life!"

He stared at me with his eyebrows raised and said, "This is a real mystery, Ruth." Then he got quiet and stare-y again.

The thing is that I know *all* about the details of my adoption, from the sudden, out-of-the-blue urgent phone call from Dad's old college roommate from medical school, to the orange vinyl seats in the waiting room, to the way that Mom cried when they found out they were getting me and had gooey mascara all over her cheeks, and the lady in charge gave Mom a tissue, but then — IN SPITE OF THE BOX OF TISSUES ON HER DESK — the lady turned her head to the side and sneezed directly into Dad's coffee. (This detail seems *paramount* to my dad. "DON'T THOSE PEOPLE KNOW HOW VIRUSES TRAVEL?") If he can remember *that*, surely he should remember more important details, like, say, the parts about *you*.

"Dad!" I shouted. "Dad! Are you in there? Answer me!"

Instead of answering me, he *touched his face*. Then his phone rang. A patient emergency, and SHAZAM! Before I could say another thing, he'd leapt out of his seat, out the front door, and into his car, and he had *zoomed* off in the direction of the hospital — which is five blocks away, and really, he should walk, as it would be better for his heart, and he of all people should know this!

I made a peanut butter sandwich because I believe that peanut butter is a perf (and delish!) food, and then carefully analyzed all that I know so far, which is:

1. I exist.
2. You exist.
3. Dad touched his face.

I know from the mighty Internet (Wikipedia!) and from reading mystery novels when I was young that people touch their faces when they lie. They also do it when they have a mite or other small bug on their skin, or have recently received an accidental eye injury. We can't be sure which one fits this scenario!

This is completely crazy and exciting, isn't it? Exciting and also *terrifically* upsetting, like being punched in the gut by a clown holding particularly interesting balloons. I actually *hate* balloons. They have so much potential to pop and be startling, causing your heart to stop from the shock, killing you instantly! As such, I can't imagine why ANYONE would give one to a small child or old person. Or me.

Coincidentally, I have this thing on the Internet that's called nopoppingballoons.tumblr.com, where I sometimes put up my poems. You can look at it if you want. I know what you're probably thinking: Who writes poems? Who *reads* poems? No one, that's who! But I *like* poems. I'm kind of a little crazy about them. I have about a hundred different books of poetry on my bookshelf and not really any novels because I just like poems. Reading them AND writing them. For me, writing poems is kind of like when you stick a needle into a blister so that the goo can run out of it before it becomes infected and spreads to your whole body, eventually killing you. I.e., they can save your life.

Mostly when I'm writing a poem, I don't even know what I'm feeling. I just start typing and BAM, next thing you know, there is the heavy weight of sadness pulling me underwater, or whoooosh, suddenly I'm light like feathers, floating up. And like magic, there are all these words on the screen. When I read them afterward, I sometimes don't even exactly remember writing them. Is that super weird? Jedgar says that maybe I'm channeling the spirit of a dead poet, but Jedgar can be insanely imaginative and also believes enthusiastically in ghosts and channeling and pretty much every other thing that most people don't believe in, such as the Loch Ness Monster and sasquatches. He's crazy, but ALSO an amazeballs animator and creative genius, so I cut him some slack. You should see another of his movies, *Butterfly Death Squad*. So beautiful AND creepily terrifying! Google it!

I have never ever ever told anyone that I have a tumblr, except Jedgar, but best friends don't count. (Sometimes I feel like I know Jedgar so well, it's like he's an extra organ, like a bonus spleen or an extra set of kidneys. Of course, then he does something upsettingly weird, like *wanting to kiss me*. Then I think he is not at all like a spare lung, but much more like ringworm or something you can only get rid of with a lot of ointment.) Anyway, the tumblr is private, in the way that things are private when you post them on the Internet for anyone to see, but only if they know where to look, and of course, no one does. So it's like a secret that isn't a secret. Like a secret that someone could find, if they really wanted to.

I thought you should see it. You know, without having to actually find it by guessing. Because you *are* me. And I *am* you. Science says so, so it must be true.

Love,

Ruth "Not A Weirdo Internet Stalker Or Other Creepy Bad Guy" Quayle

---

FROM: **Jedgar Allen Johnston**   JedgarAllenPoe@yahoo.com

TO: **Ruth Quayle**   iamruthquayle@gmail.com

Hey, so I came to your house and no one was there so I let myself in with the key that was under the mat. I left some clay on your desk. Caleb kept licking me, so I thought he was probably hungry, so I gave him some cheese. But then I remembered how cheese gives him diarrhea, so I put him outside in the yard so you wouldn't get in trouble if he ruined your mom and dad's carpet again. Sorry. He really likes cheese! No wonder he's so huge.

Can you make a bunch of SHORCAs with the clay? Because it turns out sculpting is totally hard for me. I can't make them look like actual shark/orcas, so I drew some (attached) so you can see what I need. You're good at stuff like that. Way better than me.

I don't know if *SHORCA!* needs dialogue or if we do it like a music video, cartoon-style, but with voice-overs. The dialogue you wrote sort of didn't work. At all. (And I get it about the boyfriend-girlfriend thing, so don't mention it like EVER AGAIN, thanks, not even in the script. If I got embarrassed about things like that, I'd be embarrassed, but actually, I just don't want to talk about it anymore.) Can you write the stuff for the narrator to say, like we talked about? I'm going to draw the backgrounds like I did with *Zippy* so it doesn't matter where we film the water parts. We can use the bathtub, or the toilet, if it needs to look like a whirlpool, which might be cool.

Mike and Spike are having a farting contest in my room. It's like living in a cage at the zoo where bonobos are flinging their poop and laughing. How are they my brothers? If you glued their brains together, then in total, they'd have the same IQ as one of these LEGO guys that they just threw at my screen.

. . .

Oh, great. So then right after I typed that, they dragged me to the bathroom and flushed my head in the toilet. I nearly drowned. I probably have botulism or whatever you get from toilets. Why is this my life? They will regret this when I'm a famous moviemaker. I have to go dry my hair. CALL me when you are home. I want to get out of here. Did Ruby Starling answer the email yet?

Waiting is
the worst
hardest
thing.
Time stretches
and yawns,
lazy,
a dog lying
on the couch,
wiggling his
back leg
in a dog dream
that just goes on
and on,
no end in sight,
no matter how
much the dog
tries to force out

his sleep-muted
frantic
barks.

It's hot.
I'm waiting.
The dog sleeps.

I scream
impatiently,
but only
on the inside,
while
my hands make
whole pods of whales
out of clay.

Ruby to Nan

Dear Nan,

The crash was a big canvas falling over in Mum's studio. It was
the painting that we always called the Big Baby. I know that
anything could have tipped it, like a spider dropping on it from
the ceiling and just weighing enough to topple it over. Or an

earthquake! We don't get those, but we COULD. (I don't think any one part of the planet gets to say, no, sorry, earthquakes just aren't for us.)

But that picture was propped up there for yonks, for as long as I could remember! Why would it suddenly tip?

I've been thinking about it and thinking about it and I was just lying here and counting carrots in my head, like you taught me to do when I couldn't sleep, because carrots are much more boring than sheep. And while I was counting, I was sort of thinking *you* knocked that painting over right when you did because you were answering what I wrote, weren't you? I know you did it just like I know anything that I know, like how I know Nate is the One and how I know what Mum means to say even when she forgets to say anything at all.

You did it on purpose. I know you did. Because I picked it up and propped it back on the stand and it fell down AGAIN.

It can't have happened twice, just like that. Not without the paintings all around it tipping too. It doesn't make sense!

It's scaring me a bit, that's the truth. I don't know what you're trying to tell me. I'm sorry I'm so thick. But I promise I'll keep trying to figure it out, maybe instead of counting carrots. But in the meantime, could you please stop crashing things about? Mum's still not home and I can't call Fi because if her dad answers, well... He already thinks I shouldn't be alone, even if the neighbours are close and I'm 12. It's totally legal. And I am completely fine with it, and — like you used to say! — very grown-up for my age. You'd probably be disappointed if I got all babyish and weepy just because a picture fell (TWICE!), especially if you did it on purpose from the Other Side and I was just too daft to know why.

Maybe Fi's dad is right and I should take self-defence. But I don't like hitting and kicking and those sorts of things and I don't think you can hit or kick a ghost. Besides — and I'd never tell Fi this — I think the Mole fancies me. Because of . . . well, you know, I s'pose, if you're a ghost and can see everything. And Nan, it was just a mistake. He's a total minger. I know he's Fi's brother, but she'd agree. Why do such awful boys always take an interest in me and none of the cute ones? I'm not boy-crazy, not half, but still, it might be nice if someone I liked actually liked me back. Not that it matters, I suppose, because I do know that Nate is the One. My One, that is.

I don't know why I'm still writing. I should get back into bed and keep trying to fall asleep, just to be able to stop thinking, just for a bit, especially about what you might have been trying to say by dropping the Big Baby. I know you never liked it, because you said it was sad and grey, and who would want to stare at that above their fireplace all day when they could have a pretty sunset or a jar of sunflowers or the like? But you're wrong about that. It's a nice one of Mum's, even if it's a bit creepy with all the dust and cobwebs painted up in the corners, and then in the centre, me, lying there in my cot, all lovely and cosy, and another version of me crawling out the door, all skinny and strange looking.

Oh!

NAN.

Another one of me!

A double.

A TWIN.

Nan. I'll be back in a minute. I have to stop writing and think properly. I can always sleep tomorrow.

Love,

Ruby

Ruby to Nan

Dear Nan,

Now it's morning. Mum must have stayed up all night, working in town. I've been sitting here, listening to the sounds of things bumping and the house creaking and feeling frightened, but also a bit less alone now that I think you're actually here. And I may be slow to even WANT to understand, but I know you are trying to make it as clear as the second baby in the painting that this 'Ruth' is telling the truth! It can't be a coincidence that there are scads of paintings and sculptures and things where there are almost always two of me.

I just don't quite want to believe it, Nan.

My stomach is going funny. If it's true, then it means that

Mum *knows*. You can't have two babies pop out of you and not know. But you were there when I was born! So you knew too. You KNEW. You both did.

So it's ... true?

It's true.

I can't explain why, not really, but I do *feel* like it's true. That's such a strange thing to say, and I'd never say it aloud, but I daresay writing to a dead person is as much a secret journal as anything. It's true. Not just because she looks exactly like me, but with a not-very-good haircut. Not just because she's right about the birthday and the hospital and that. But it's true because when I saw her picture, something settled inside me, like something small shifting and clicking into its proper place. I think I was *hoping* it was a stalker because that seemed less complicated. I don't like things to be complicated. I like them to be simple. Then I can cope, and so can Mum.

But Nan, mostly I'm FURIOUS. It just isn't the sort of thing you hide from a person, you know! A twin? It just isn't. What is *wrong* with both of you?

I am 12. And even though Mum took me to that lecture on "How to Cope With Unexpected Stress" last May for our mini-break in Scotland, I have no idea what to do with this! I'll look at the notes from that, in case there really are useful tips after all, but I think the point was that some things you just *can't* cope with, and Nan, I don't think I can cope with this.

Don't try to tell me anything else. Please don't. I don't want to be scared out of my wits when you knock over the microwave or push me down the stairs.

Ruby

PS — Still love you and miss you, though, Nan. So much.

FROM: **Ruth Quayle** iamruthquayle@gmail.com

TO: **Jedgar Allen Johnston** JedgarAllenPoe@yahoo.com

Ruby Starling hasn't answered my reply to her rude brush-off. I am *super* upset. Should I write to her again? Should I see if I can somehow find a phone number for her and *call* her? Should I *totes freak out*? Or tell Dad that I actually wrote to her and demand that he do something?

This is the craziest thing that has ever happened to anyone ever at any time in the history of all of mankind! How can I go on, knowing my twin is OUT THERE and not answering my heartfelt notes? WHAT DO I DO NEXT?

Anyway, I'm home now! Come over ASAP. Climb the trellis, like always — do NOT use the front door. And knock on the window four times fast and four times slow, so I know it's you. I'm making SHORCAs like crazy. All these thoughts careening around my head are giving me as much energy as that time I drank a cappuccino at Starbucks just to see what it was like. I've already done four! How many do you think we'll need?

FROM: **Gen Quayle** `Gen@usdinolab.org`

TO: **Ruth Quayle** `iamruthquayle@gmail.com`

Hi Sweetie!

I am so sorry, I have to stay a couple of extra days here in Beantown to meet with the media. This is getting more attention than I thought! Hope it turns into grant money. (I bought you a great Harvard decal for your skateboard!)

Did you hear me on NPR? I thought about you listening, which is why I made that joke about T. rex. But now I suspect all the news agencies will focus on T. rex, and again not on the Luffster. I can't get grants if no one cares about the Luffster specifically. Poor Luffy. Why don't they see how cool he is? And how cool *cloning* is? At least, of dinosaurs. They all want to talk about people-cloning, and the ethics of that, which makes me crazy because it's nothing to do with dinosaur cloning, which could be an amazing, amazing breakthrough, for obvious reasons! I'm sure we're only a decade away from being able to clone anything in a lab, but no one is going to ever go for the human angle, I don't think. At least, I hope not. That's up to nature to take care of, with monozygotic twins, which really — if you think about it — are natural clones and not so very different from what we're doing, apart from . . .

Oh, you don't care about this either, do you, Ruth? You're 12! Sometimes I forget that it would be completely age-appropriate for you to care way more about things like friends and boys and your other hobbies and interests than about cloning prehistoric animals for science. (Although, tell Jedgar that if he could make a dinosaur movie about the Luffster, I'd really appreciate the rise in its popularity!)

Do you want to have a spa day when I get back? I know you think manicures are "totes lame," but it could actually be fun if you give it a chance. We could have facials. I've never had one because I hate the idea of a stranger rubbing her hands all over my face, but the in-flight magazine said beauty rituals are a great mommy-and-me activity. Maybe you and I should do more of those things and less talking about my job, which should be on the periphery of your life and not take over everything (including the dining room!) for your whole adolescence. Do you remember when you were little and you used to leave food out for Luffetta every night? That was so cute. We eventually had to tell you to leave dog food because Caleb was eating it all and getting terribly overweight, the pig.

Want to Skype later? I'm happy to talk to you about anything, you know that, right? Especially if you have ideas for our summer trip! It's already July, and we haven't chosen a destination yet! (Let's you and I choose it and then surprise your dad, OK?) Your last note made me think you've got an awful lot going on in that brain of yours. If it's Skype-worthy, then I'll be back at the hotel by 9 at the latest. Did you remember to take your medication? Dad may be a doctor, but I worry that he's not good at reminding you. Take your meds!

And please please please try to help Daddy with dinner and stuff. You know how he is. Give him a kiss from me and then tell him to give you one from me to you. Miss you lots! Love you more than fruit dunked in a chocolate fountain!

Mommy

FROM: Ruth Quayle iamruthquayle@gmail.com

TO: Gen Quayle Gen@usdinolab.org

Mom,

Please stop signing off as "Mommy." You know I love you, but I'm only weeks (OK, weeks AND then a few more weeks) away from becoming a teenager, and we both need to get used to that idea. I thought we agreed that "Mom" was OK but "Mother" was not because it sounds too formal, like something someone in a scary movie would call his mom right before he turned into a zombie and tried to eat her brain. So from now on, you are MOM, OK? Just Mom.

I can't talk about this Top Secret Matter of Relative Urgency on Skype or email. No way! I need you and Dad (not DADDY) to be sitting in the same room, looking me square in the eye. I might see if I can borrow a lie detector thing from somewhere too. Do you know where I could get one? It's not that I don't trust you guys. I just feel like you will be more honest if you know an alarm will go off and a shock will be administered if you lie to me during this fact-finding mission.

I think cloning the Luffster is a pretty cool, amazing, unbelievable thing, Mom. I know that outside of movies, the dinosaurs wouldn't all start stomping around in the park or whatnot and instead would be kept in lab incubators for all time, but still, it would eventually be a terrific sequel to SHORCA!

By the way, have you talked to Dad about . . . anything? Did he say anything about anything? At all? Just asking. And why did you mention TWINS?

I love you! And don't worry about anything, I never forget my meds. How can I forget? I've taken them every day of my life. That would be like forgetting to brush my teeth, but different, because actually I have forgotten to brush once or twice.

Love you more than clouds shaped like poltergeists,
Ruth

There are two things:
True things.
And lies.
When you figure out
which is which
it's like you are on the inside
of the balloon
looking out,
seeing the pin coming toward you
in the sunlight
but not being able
to move away.

Or maybe,
the thing is
that all of us are
two people:
the one inside
the balloon.
And the one
holding
the pin.

Holy cow, srsly, Ruth, those clay SHORCAs you made are amazing. You're super extra good at this. Better than writing even. It's basically like sculpture is your secret talent. Claymation is hard and it's SO much easier to draw stuff, but these are the best things ever, so I want to figure out a way to do both. Like you know how most of our movies are just you writing the words and me doing drawings? When we add the sculpted SHORCAs, it's like just as much your project as mine.

FROM: **David Quayle** docdaddave@gmail.com

TO: **Ruth Quayle** iamruthquayle@gmail.com

Hi honey,
Heading home now. Up for a walk? I bet you forgot to walk Caleb. Besides, it's finally cooled off out here. And if you're not asleep, walking is the best cure for insomnia! I read about it in the doctors' lounge while I was waiting for

the OR and trying to stay awake last Tuesday night. I'm pretty sure that boredom is actually the best cure for insomnia, but I'm not that kind of doctor.

I just realized that I didn't answer your question the other day about the agency, so I wanted to tell you that I sent them an email requesting another look at your file. It was a closed adoption, though, honey, so I don't think it's really possible.

Anyway, I thought we could talk about it on our walk. Maybe don't mention it to Mom yet. I think it might be hard for her, emotionally, to know that you're searching for your birth mother, even if you're not. Are you? It's just that last time we talked about it, you said that you hated your birth mother and never wanted to find her because you could never forgive her. I know you love us, but I also know — because I am old and wise! — that there is a part of you that's still upset that you were given up. Which is fine, Rooty. All adopted kids probably feel that to some extent. It's just that — are you sure about opening up this whole Pandora's box? If you want to do it, you should do it! It's fine. We're grown-ups and we can handle it. I just want to make sure that you are up for it. Because I'm your dad, I don't want you to get hurt.

I'll figure out how to tell your mom about your quest. And even if she's sad, she'll still get it. She's pretty smart. That's why I picked her. ☺

But Ruth, my girl, I think the look-alike is just a case of coincidental facial features, I really do. They would have *had* to tell us, if not legally, then morally.

Love,

Daddy

Sent from my iPhone

FROM: **Ruth Quayle** iamruthquayle@gmail.com

TO: **David Quayle** docdaddave@gmail.com

Sure, let's go for a walk. I'm totally awake still! Jedgar just left an hour ago. We were working on the stuff for *SHORCA!* I've talked him out of doing the voice part in French, mostly because neither of us speaks French, and it turns out that French sounds ultra awkward when you say it out loud with terrible American accents. We're using Spanish instead. *¡Mira! ¡Un tiburón! ¡Eso se ve como una ballena! ¡Ayuda!* It sounds totes excellent and super dramatic and very, very emotional, see? We're still not sure how it will come together, but Jedgar says that's normal, that at first when you are making a movie, everything is all over the place and it's like you've put it into a blender and ground it all up to the point where you don't even know what your original idea was, but then something CLICKS and it all comes together. 'Course things you put in the blender don't actually come together again, so never mind.

I am *not* looking for my birth mother. I am furious with her and I will never forgive her, etc., never mind what Buddha says. You know yourself that Buddha lived a million years ago or whatever and knows nothing about what it feels like to have been adopted. Buddha also would have been mad about it if it happened to him. Who GIVES AWAY A BABY? Babies are not like zucchinis, where you grow extras and foist the rest on your neighbors and act insulted when they say, "No, thank you." I want *nothing* to do with my birth mother. I am merely on a journey of self-discovery after finding my twin. It's not just that I found a sister, it's that it makes me someone's twin! It changes ME too. Don't you see? It's a different thing.

Mom is still Mom. You are still you. I am still me. Caleb is still Caleb and I wish he would get off my lap. (Google should offer a translation service to dog language, so I could tell him that 90 pounds is too heavy to impose on other people's legs.) NOTHING IS GOING TO CHANGE, except for the fact that I have a twin sister named Ruby Starling who possibly believes that I am a crazy person stalking her on the Internet.

See you in a minute. DO NOT TYPE AND DRIVE. And you are DAD, not DADDY. It's very hard to communicate to you people that I am NO LONGER A BABY.

Love,
Ruth

FROM: **David Quayle** docdaddave@gmail.com

TO: **Ruth Quayle** iamruthquayle@gmail.com

OK, OK.
Love,
Daddy
Sent from my iPhone

FROM: **David Quayle** docdaddave@gmail.com

TO: **Ruth Quayle** iamruthquayle@gmail.com

See what I did there? Did you laugh?
Love,
Dad
Sent from my iPhone

ROFLMAO, Dad. Or, as they would say in Spanish, *riendo el culo*!

P.S. Google Translate is the bomb.

P.P.S. Are you emailing me from the driveway? Weirdo.

Ruby to Nan

Dear Nan,

I had to write back because I'm sorry. I feel terrible being angry with you when you're dead. It's just that I got so upset about the haunting that you tried to do. It was sweet, really. I'm sure you meant it to be kind. But it was also terrifying. Couldn't you just write a note or arrange the letter magnets on the fridge in a meaningful way? Not that we've got letter magnets, but I will get some if you think you could actually do that. Or no. Never mind. Obviously dead people don't rearrange letter magnets! If they could, everyone would do it! All those fridges would be full of spooky messages from the Other Side.

The thing with writing letters to people who are dead is that it's sort of like they are as good as sent as soon as you've written them. You can't exactly crumple them up and discard them. The ghost might've been reading over your shoulder the whole time! So if you did read that last note, the furious one, well, I'm sorry. You can haunt me. I am OK with it. (I think. At least I'll try to be.) Just don't do anything too horror-film. You know I hate horror films.

Love,

Ruby

FROM: **Ruby Starling** starling_girl@mail.com

TO: **Fiona** fififionafifi@aol.co.uk

Fi, I know you think it's mad, but I have been studying these pics of 'Ruth', trying to figure out what the Photoshopped bits are. Because you can always tell what's been edited, right? There's sometimes a smidge of blue where there shouldn't be. Or a line is smooth when it should be bumpy. And there just *aren't* any things like that wrong with these photos.

See, she's a bit different from me, after all. Her face is long and narrowish and more goat-y. My front teeth are gappy. Her eyes are squintier. She looks quite a bit *smaller.* I know you can do that with Photoshop — that's why celebs are always thinner and less wrinkly in pics — but wouldn't it be too much trouble? And why would she bother, really? I can see why people pretend to be giving away STOP tickets or the like in order to sneakily get you to hand over all of your life savings, but I can't quite figure out why someone would pretend to be my adopted twin in America. What d'you think?

She knows where I was born. And my birthday. And she has the ear. Nan's ear. Mum's ear. *MY* ear. I've never seen an ear like ours before on anyone else, ever! No one would edit that *in*, because I doubt anyone else would notice, not really. Just me. And Mum. And Nan.

So there's all that, which is really a lot of evidence!

But there's also . . .

What I'm trying to say is that it's been brought to my attention that . . .

I mean, I think that maybe . . .

OK, I don't know how to tell you this without you thinking I've gone and lost the plot. It's just that it's not really so much about the Photoshopping clues or the fact she knew my birth date and the place I was born (which I suppose anyone could find out, if they really looked. It's in the hospital records!) or anything like that. It's just that I think Nan's sent me a message from the Other Side!

And the message she sent is basically that what Ruth says is true. And the thing is that I think it is. It's true.

There, I said it.

I THINK IT'S TRUE, FI.

I, Ruby Starling, have a twin who lives in America!

Don't try to talk me out of it. I have loads of proof up in Mum's studio. You've seen her paintings! You know she always paints and sculpts and draws TWO girls. It's not ME x 2. It's ME AND RUTH. She's maybe been trying to tell me all along. She's maybe just been waiting for me to guess! But I didn't! I guess I must be pretty thick, after all.

Now I've said it to you, it's even more true than it was before, and my hands have started shaking like Mum's do when she's in a confrontation or stressed or even just unhappy. I suppose I have to talk to Mum now, don't I? I'm scared to, and I don't know why, not exactly. I think that if she wanted me to know, she would have told me, and there must be some reason why she hasn't. And if it wasn't something terrible, then I'd be sitting here with my TWIN SISTER RUTH instead of trying to figure out how or why she even exists.

Something's happening to me, something awful. Like nausea, except it isn't that. It's dread, filling me up, like hot tea that falls on your lap and scalds your legs through your trousers. I'm scared. Can I come round? It's just that I can't just sit here, knowing all these things, without feeling like I have to scream or do something, but I don't even know what.

Ruby

Oh, Ru-Ru, I don't believe it! I mean, it can't be real! (And yes, come round, of course!)

It's just that this is a bit mad, isn't it? How could your mum have had two of you and not told you about it? Your mum's a bit odd, sure, but she's always telling you all those details about your dad and when she found out she was going to have you and how he used to sing all these strange French rock songs that she hated to her stomach, but you loved them because you'd kick her extra hard then. She can't have left out, 'Oh, by the way, there were two babies in there, dancing together to *Le Rock et Roll*, and I left one behind in America'. She just wouldn't.

Anyway, don't you remember when I did that paper last term about art and things and I interviewed your mum and one of the questions was why did she always paint two of you? And she didn't say, 'Gosh, that's because I had twins and put one up for adoption in America and kept it a secret all these years'. Here, I've got it right in front of me on the screen. She actually said, 'Oh, that represents the duality of human nature, particularly in children, who often seem like two people at once'. Don't you remember?

And besides, that sculpture she's doing for the library square is truly JUST YOU. Not you and some bonkers girl from America who happens to be your . . . twin? That can't be.

Gosh, I've just remembered, you can't come round. I'm leaving right now to meet Chloe and Soph for Hawkster's do. I can wait for you at the end of the drive. Please come. Am sure it will be a lot more fun than it sounds. I'm a bit worried about you, actually. I feel like I shouldn't go!

FROM: **Ruby Starling**   starling_girl@mail.com

TO: **Fiona**   fififionafifi@aol.co.uk

I'm OK. Really. GO. I'm fine! Well, not FINE. I'm actually not feeling at all well, Fi. I'm just all squiggly inside, but it's nothing to worry about. I can't explain. It's like being ill without being actually ill. Can't possibly face Hawkster's. I really really really have to talk to Ruth properly.

Can you pop in anyway and take the sparkly tops that Chlophie want? I don't want to see them and have to explain why I'm not all amazeog and fab or glam or anything except really confused and upset. I just want to lie here with the lights out and maybe cry a bit, or just be so quiet and still, I might not even exist at all.

The funny thing is that now I know that I have a twin, I feel like half of me has just been peeled away, like a decal being pulled off its back sticky bit, making me just the waxy papery rubbish left behind.

Roooob, Fi says you aren't coming to Hawkster's, and we're really really *really* gutted. It's going to be a great laugh! And your clothes won't have any fun without you! Even with us in them, dancing and whatever people do at proper swish teenage parties! Pleeeease change your mind. Even if the boys just want to sit and watch the footie, we're going to bring Sophie's mum's tarot and read everyone's cards! Then 'course we'll be able to tell which of these lads is going to be our first boyfriend, right? And which ones are just useless. There should be a 'total prat' card! Anyway, it'll be soooo fab. Please come!

Oh, we have to go, Fi's here with your things. She's got an empty orange squash bottle too, so we can play Spin the Bottle. Think what you're missing! Smooch smooch smooch!

Chloe's been flossing her teeth for yonks 'cause she's scared of having smelly breath. She's chewed about ten packs of Trident. Chlo, you're being ridic! Your breath is always luverly, like flowers! Or something minty! Not DAISIES, those smell like feet! No! No one minds anyway, you silly goose. If they get to snog you, they'll be sooooo happy, they won't even notice if you've just eaten a rotten egg.

Ohhhh, lovely, these are my fav shoes of yours, and thanks SO much! You're a star! Feel better! Byeeeeee!

FROM: **Ruby Starling** starling_girl@mail.com

TO: **Ruth Quayle** iamruthquayle@gmail.com

Dear Ruth,

OK.

Fine.

OK.

I just keep saying that out loud. 'OK'. Then 'Fine'. Then 'OK' again. Then I go check my face in the mirror to make sure I'm still there. I don't expect you'll know what I mean, but sometimes I think maybe I'll look one day and I'll be gone. Just fizzled out or fogged over or faded away. Now more than ever, I feel like I'm just paper-thin, like if you held up a light behind me, you'd see right through. Not like I've found another version of me, but more that I've just realised that half of me has been torn away. Don't expect that makes sense, but it's true, because . . .

My friends will think I'm mad (I'm supposed to be at a party with them right now but stayed home to write to you!). But I, Ruby Elizabeth Starling, age 12⅔, believe you, Ruth Elizabeth Quayle, age 12⅔, are my *twin sister*.

I can't believe I'm even saying that! This is like a strange dream and soon I'm going to wake up and think, 'Gosh, that was bonkers'.

But.

Well, BUT.

It's complicated, but my nan told me. She's dead. You asked me about ghosts and, now I *do* believe in them. Because of Nan. And how she sent me this sign that you were telling the truth! Do you believe in things like that? Signs and things? I do.

I still haven't asked Mum about you. It's not that I don't want to, it's just that I can't. She's in the middle of this massive art installation for our new library. The commission was huge for her — she'd been at loose ends and having a hard time — so it's a lifesaver. Anyway, she's very intense about it all. You have to understand, that's how she is, it's how she does everything, her art especially. She just does it full on, in these big bursts of creative genius! But while she's working on something, she's . . . it's like she sort of takes leave of herself a bit. She forgets to sleep and to come home sometimes even, and she sometimes wakes me up in the middle of the night, thinking it's morning and I have to get to school, only to realise that it's nighttime and the summer hols.

She's always been that way. Nan used to say that Mum let go of the reins so long ago that her horses had time to gallop clear out of the country, never to return again. (Nan was very horsey when she was young and I think she was a bit disappointed that Mum wasn't quite so proper and ENGLISH about everything. She didn't care a bit for horses and wasn't all gaga about the Royals or the proper way to make tea or any of that.)

Nan had lots of stories about things Mum did when she was young that most people wouldn't do. Crazy things. Embarrassing things. She'd tell them sometimes when Mum wasn't around. If Mum heard her, she'd get cross, saying that Nan was confusing me or making her seem like she was incompetent, but I guess the thing is that she is a little incompetent. Not at everything, just at being a mum. But she's a brilliant artist. You should Google her. She's a bit famous-ish. Her name is Delilah Starling, but it's also Delilah Etourneau. You can find loads of things under both names.

The thing is that she usually only paints *me*, which you'll see. I wish she wouldn't, but that's not the point. The point is that the sign that Nan sent me was this one painting Mum did when I was a baby. It's skin-crawlingly creepy, because there's me in my cot, sleeping, and then in the shadowy corner of the room, there's *another* me, crawling towards the door.

Nan knocked the painting over! To tell me something! And I think she wanted me to know that it's *you*, the baby crawling towards the door! It's not the duality of humankind or whatever Fi said that Mum told her for her essay. It's YOU. Ruth Quayle. Leaving us.

It's *shivery* to think that, isn't it? I shivered, typing it out.

But it all almost fits, if only it made sense. I *was* born in New York City. Mum and Dad were living there at the time. Mum says New York was the best place on earth for an artist to live, and Dad wanted to become a famous actor. It was so romantic! They were young and in love and newly-wed and had a flat so small that the bath was in the living room. Mum was getting ready to do a show at one of their friends' galleries and Dad was making money being a waiter at a French restaurant and going on all sorts of glamorous auditions and trying to learn how to speak American English properly so he wasn't always rejected for being so French.

And then he DIED.

I don't like to talk about that too much, even though I didn't ever know him. It's just so tragic though, being young and in love and running away to America for fame and fortune, and then getting hit by a cab while crossing the road.

Mum says she couldn't believe it either. She says she would sit in the bathtub in the middle of the flat she couldn't afford anymore and wait for him to come in the door, all the while getting bigger and bigger and bigger with me, until she had to stop taking baths because she was afraid she'd get stuck. (She had sponge baths instead, of course. Not that she stayed dirty.)

Then I was born. I guess it was terribly upsetting because she doesn't say much about it except that her water broke right outside Saks Fifth Avenue and the doorman there was lovely and hailed her a cab right away and even paid for it because she couldn't afford to do it. Someone at the hospital called Nan and she came whisking over efficiently from England, even though she and Mum hadn't spoken for yonks, because of the whole 'moving to America with my French husband even though we are very young' situation, which Nan didn't approve of. And then she moved back to England with me — and missed out on her fab American show, after all! — to live with Nan, who is really the only person that Mum would allow to help her out. And she needed help. She was very depressed, and it's hard to be a mum. She tells me all the time how she didn't think she could do it, but she did, because Nan was there telling her to get out of bed in the morning and things like that. Nan was the most lovely, amazing woman in the world.

I don't have any other rellies. Dad's family all live in France, and I think they hate Mum, because they think he moved to New York for Mum, for her art, and then got killed. Which she says is rubbish, he moved to America for his own career! So that's totally unfair of them to be cruel to her about it, but they've never liked the English for some confusing reason that Mum says has to do with something that happened a hundred years ago. I don't take it personally. They are obviously really really really strange people who hold grudges and don't like England at all. And I'm English! I get lovely French cards from them on my birthday and at Christmas, when they write me things in French because they don't speak English (or just refuse to try, says Mum). My French is terrible so mostly I just admire the nice Frenchness of the stylish stationery and then put them in a box under my bed and don't ever answer them. So I can't write to them now. How would you say, 'Why do I have a twin I don't know about? Love, your barbarian English granddaughter' in French?

About a year after Dad died, Mum changed her last name to Starling, because it's the English translation of 'Etourneau'. (That was his name, Philippe Etourneau.) She wanted to keep his name, but she was so angry with his French family that she didn't want to keep *their* name. So it's really all a huge mix-up of hurt feelings and misunderstandings and things, like a pantomime, except not even a bit funny.

I am honestly terrible at French. I think maybe that's part of why I feel like Dad is only a story to me — not quite real. I just don't feel FRENCH. Mum says I got my sense of style from Dad, but I don't know. I don't think style is a thing you can inherit from someone dead, and in the pictures, his clothes aren't really that special. He was astonishingly handsome, though. Like, pop-star handsome. I can see why Mum loved him.

Now that Nan's gone, it's just Mum and me. Sometimes she has boyfriends, but they're mostly smug gits. Dad probably was one too, if you think about it. If all her boyfriends now are awful, why would he be the one who was different just because he's dead? And French? I try not to think about that a lot, because I want to like my dad, even if he is dead and French and I'll never meet him. Unless heaven is real, then I suppose I'll meet him there, but he won't know me, will he? And even thinking about all that gives me a migraine, so I really mustn't talk about it anymore. Besides, it's more than you want to know, I'm sure.

I don't know why I'm telling you all this! None of it adds up to anything. And I just don't understand how you were adopted and I'm not. Definitely not. I have a photo of my mum when she was up the duff, so I know for sure that I'm hers. She was *huge*, like a baleen whale. (Normally she's rake thin, even when she eats nothing but chips and tea for weeks, like she does when she's working.) In the photo, there's a plate and cup balanced there on her stomach. She says it was just like a shelf where she could store things, like car keys and snacks and her mobile phone. She once found a bar of chocolate that she'd been eating hidden in there half a day later, all melted and squished into her skin. She says it must have fallen down her blouse and she hadn't noticed. She was so sad then, you see, she didn't notice a lot of things. She says it was all a blur of being sad and huge and pretending to be OK, even when she wasn't, just so her show could go on, which it didn't ever do. It makes me sad to think about that! How hard she worked and then I came along at just the wrong time.

Anyway, I look just like her, except for having Dad's hair and the gappy thing between my front teeth. Mum has this marvelously glamorous red hair that cascades all down her back in perfect curls. Up until I was five, I was sure she was a mermaid, but then Nan convinced me of how silly that was, as obviously mermaids are fairy tales and also, Mum can't swim.

I have to have a think. It takes me awhile to think about things. Mum is always saying, 'Ruby is a thinker'! Can you stop writing to me, just for a few days? While I think. It's just that you say so much in your notes that I get muddled up and can't straighten it all out properly in my head.

Dear Ruby,

YAY! I got your note and I actually whooped out loud and clapped. Also, just like that, after days of feeling like my legs couldn't stay still, they stopped jiggling.

YES, RUBY.

YES.

IT'S TRUE.

WE ARE TWINS!

I am so so so so so so so so so happy that you know, that you understand. That we are *right*. That we are us. And we're so much alike! I like thinking too. And I get migraines. And I totes get what you're saying about checking the mirror to see if you're still there. I've always felt like that! But I thought it was because I was adopted, so I was missing all the strings that attach regular people to the earth, so I always felt floaty and like I was different from everyone else and kind of fainter and sort of transparent compared to them, like they were solid and real and I was just . . . an illusion. Something that someone made up.

I SO GET IT, RUBY! I DO!

Mom got delayed in Boston so she's not coming back until late *tonight*, but after that, I will have ANSWERS.

I can hardly type this because my hands are shaking and my mind is whirling like a dervish. I'm just . . . I know you're thinking, but I have to say this part and I hope it doesn't give you a headache or confuse you, but it's just so huge and true and important that I can't not say it.

RUBY, IF YOU ARE NOT ADOPTED, THEN YOUR PARENTS ARE MY PARENTS.

My "real" parents.

If you are not adopted, then maybe you do not know how huge this news is when you are adopted and then discover a twin on the Internet and then accidentally — because you weren't thinking about ever even wanting to find your Real Parents™ — you find out who they are. It's like everything you ever wanted or dreamed about, all crunched up into a boulder-sized snowball and thrown at your face unexpectedly, dislodging your front teeth.

It's almost too much to take in. And it hurts.

A lot.

What you say is just, well, honestly, it's NOT what I was imagining when I imagined who my real parents were. When I was a little kid, I thought they were probably super-famous people, possibly royalty, and that maybe I had to be given away because I needed to be a boy for the good of the country somehow. But then when I got older and more mature and saw some daytime talk shows, I figured out that doesn't really happen, and it's more likely that they were frail or poor or teenagers or some combo of all three, and I was sad. I mourned the king and queen who gave me away to save the Kingdom of Cornucopia! But then I got around to feeling sad for my tragic teen parents and imagined that they had gone on to college and were some-day going to find me and hug me and tell me they loved me and whatnot, even though they had to give me away because they were poor and young and (possibly) mysteriously sick, with something historical-sounding and romantic-ish, like consumption. When I tried to picture them, the image got all blurry around the edges and swam out of my line of sight. So that's sort of as far as I got when I was imagining it, to the hug. And then . . . that was it.

Then I turned twelve and I realized that my parents were just people who decided not to keep me, and I got mad. Dad says that being angry makes people sick, and I've already had enough of sicknesses for my whole life, so I know he's just trying to protect me from getting sick again by teaching me all this stuff about Buddhism. He says it saved his life, a long time ago, but sometimes I think he just likes Buddhism when it makes him feel like he's right about things. And he might be right about being angry, but that doesn't mean that I'm *not* angry. There's no other way of look-ing at it anyway, Ruby. Someone, somewhere, *gave me away*.

And I guess, if you're right, and you weren't adopted after all, then YOUR MOM, Delilah Starling, is the one. She is the one who gave me away. So obviously, all my rage about being given away suddenly has a place to go, and that's square onto her shoulders. I'm sorry, but it's true. In Buddhism, in case you don't know this, there are Four Noble Truths, and the gist of them is that even though life is generally pretty miserable, you can make yourself happier by being in the moment and not being really super angry with people from your past and so on. (It's quite confusing.) And I know that I am not going to be filled with inner peace and such because my insides are basically a giant, white squall of fury. That doesn't fit with ANYTHING in Buddhism, but I don't care. I can't believe she gave me away.

And she kept you?

I just can't make it make sense.

And honestly, now I'm sort of angry with you too, even though it's not your fault, but not at your dad because it's not his fault that he's dead!

When I used to picture anything about my Real Mom™, I just imagined long graceful hands and hair that shone golden in the sunlight and a small smiling mouth. Then, like I said, I got furious with her. After that, I pictured her as someone who chewed gum aggressively and didn't brush her hair and maybe had terrible teeth and spat when she talked. But I just couldn't put the pieces together to make a whole person, you know?

Someone awful.

But now I guess I can just Google her.

This is so surreal, it's like you can't even begin to make it seem real in your head. In my head, I mean. Maybe it doesn't seem so weird to you.

I don't know why I can't seem to bring myself to enter her name in the search bar! But I can't. Oh, my heart is beating so fast, it's like wings. I don't like it. I'm freaking out.

I'm completely and totally freaking out.

It's weird.

Upsetting.

Anyway, you can't possibly get what I mean.

Because you are the one she kept.

And now I'm crying really, really hard. It's bubbling out of me like an erupting volcano of molten tears! I have to stop typing.

I have to think too.

Mostly right now, I think that I hope I'm wrong. Because even when I was mad all the time at this *idea* of a mom, that was nothing compared to how it feels to be mad at an actual person with long red hair and an inability to tell night from day when she's working.

Love,

Ruth

I want to say that I'm sorry about your dad. I didn't say it before, but I should have because your dad died and I AM sorry. I know you seem not very sad about it but I think you must be sad, deep down inside, and not really just annoyed with his French relatives, who DO sound annoying, if only because they don't seem to care about you, and it's awful to not feel cared about. I know that. Not because my parents don't care about me, but because I don't think many people care about me, really — just my parents and Jedgar. Sometimes it's like I live on an island. An Island of Ruth, where I'm just entirely alone. And Mom and Dad and Jedgar come and visit and it's totes fun and happy and awesome when they do. But the rest of the time, I'm on the island alone with birds and squirrels and whatnot, but feeling like I just don't quite fit.

But the truth is, I'm never alone. Because of Ashley Mary Jane.

I have to tell you about AMJ RIGHT NOW, before I get too mad at you to tell you things that you should know.

I know it's a lot to take in, especially on top of this crazy revelation about Delilah Starling, child abandoner. But I have to tell you this because if you don't know this, then you can't be on my island. Do you know what I mean? There are things only people on your island can know and you're my twin, so you have to be on my island with me. And if I don't tell you now, then when I do tell you, you'll feel walloped by it, just like I feel walloped by the mermaid Delilah.

I have someone else's heart.

My heart used to belong to a baby named Ashley Mary Jane McNay. She died when she was 1⅙ years old, in a car wreck in upstate New York. Her parents were named Haley and Jack McNay. It was raining. They were on their way to Costco when their car was smashed to smithereens by a pickup truck (silver, with patches of rust). No one else died, but her mom had three broken ribs and her dad is still in a wheelchair. Her brother was completely and totally entirely fine! He's 17 now and his name is Chaz. I sometimes pretend that he's my brother, even though he's not, and basically I only see him one time per year. Chaz plays varsity football, or did last year. He is extremely cute, Hollywood-level cute. Basically, he looks exactly like what an older brother would look like on TV. Like he was made to be someone's hero! To save the day! Etc.! And so on!

I needed a heart because of all the holes in mine. There are pictures of me in the NICU (Neonatal Intensive Care Unit) where I look exactly like a frog, splayed out on a dissecting tray, but with a biggish (compared to my body) baby head. My limbs were all blueish and not regular flesh-colored, which is how I know my situation was totes dire, if the spindly limbs and tubes didn't give it away. They put in Ashley Mary Jane's heart, and threw my miniature Swiss cheese heart, full of holes and airy parts, directly into the trash, or the "medical waste" as Dad likes to say when I remind him that my heart is in the landfill. (It's not! They burn medical waste. My poor old heart.) I miss my old heart sometimes, like you might miss a teddy bear you had when you were a baby.

I was a month old when I had the operation. Only ONE MONTH!

I *should* have died, I guess. Maybe a whole bunch of times. It's complicated, but I think that if I wasn't about to die, Mom and Dad wouldn't have got me. They got me BECAUSE of my heart and how Dad was a heart surgeon. And because I guess they were told that it was a legal technicality and I'd die anyway. Mom says she knew I'd live, even though they had to revive me with tiny CPR paddles and air tubes and machines that were as big as airplanes next to my baby-bird body. Can you even imagine? Every time I see a fresh new wrinkly red baby in the mall, gurgling and spitting up in its stroller, I can't help but imagine it being dead and then revived, and then I get choked up with a wave of weeping that could flood the entire store. Poor babies. Poor baby me. Poor everyone.

So I am only *not* dead because a driver in a silver truck was drunk and smashed right into Ashley Mary Jane, who was not meant to be dead. She was in the wrong place at the wrong time, but it was the right place for me, because if she hadn't been there, I wouldn't be here. What a terrible trade, right? What if you were Ashley Mary Jane's brother? Boy, he must hate me.

Anyway, what if I was born to be dead? And she wasn't? It's like we mixed everything up, the way things were supposed to be. But what does that mean, "supposed to be"? It's like what people say to Mom all the time about cloning a dinosaur that is extinct: "Maybe they are *supposed* to be extinct. Maybe you are messing with the natural order." And then she says, "That's the point, that we can mess with it. And there's so much to learn."

And then I think, OK, maybe I am here because I have so much to learn! And then I try harder at school. School is sort of actually really really really hard for me, but I work extra hard because I feel like I should, because I am not dead and Ashley Mary Jane is. I sometimes set my alarm and do extra studying at night when Mom and Dad are sleeping so I can stay at the gifted school and they will think I am smart, and then everyone who knows about me and Ashley Mary Jane won't think that her heart went to waste.

After my surgery, Mom and Dad told Ashley Mary Jane's parents right away that they could keep in touch with us, so they would know how their daughter's heart was making someone else have this amazing life. So I kind of *owe* them an amazing life.

Every year, we meet Ashley Mary Jane's parents at this huge event called the Walk to Remember. It's always in a different town, but there's always a big field and what we do is we take all these balloons, a different color every year, and we tie notes to them, and we send them up to Ashley Mary Jane. Other people send balloons to their own dead kids, and then everyone cries, and it sounds AWFUL and so sad, but it's kind of amazing and beautiful. Then we have salmon and bagels and lemonade with the McNays and hang around and listen to music, and then at the end, Mom and Dad hug the McNays and I get hugged by them so hard they nearly squeeze my (her) heart clear out of my body, and then everyone cries a little more and sniffs and says, "Have a good year!" Chaz sometimes doesn't say anything. Last year, he had his earphones in the whole time. But Mom says that's normal, that he's a teenage boy and he probably just isn't sure entirely how to act.

It's all sort of like our New Year's Eve, except it happens in August and it's usually painfully hot, no matter whether it's in Idaho or Maine or wherever. On the way home, we are always very quiet and we listen to the air conditioner or the plane's engine and think about Ashley Mary Jane, and I feel her heart thumping away in my chest and feel lucky to be alive and weirdly happy and full of love for her and her family and my family and basically all the families. The whole thing is a lovefest, in the best possible way that is also the saddest thing.

That feeling doesn't last long. Like, I don't walk around all the time going, "GOSH, I LOVE EVERYONE!" That would be totes weird. I'm just telling YOU all this because I feel like YOU will understand.

You have to.

Anyway, I sometimes think maybe I'm more likely to die sooner than other people because I'm here on borrowed time, and Death is getting ultra-annoyed that I got away so many times before I was even one year old. I *try* not to be freaked out by this. I *try* to think about how I'll be a ghost and can haunt everyone who ever made me mad, like Freddie Blue Anderson, who is this horrible girl at my school with perfect hair and a super-extra-lousy personality.

I don't really think I'll die *soon*. My policy is, REFUSE TO BE AFRAID. (And stay in the present! Like Buddha!) Being dead doesn't seem like something to be afraid of, anyway, whether you believe in heaven or an afterlife or just nothingness. Death is something that happens to everyone at some time or another! You probably don't know when it's happening to you, so what does it matter? I just don't want to miss stuff like my first kiss and seeing every scary movie ever made and graduating and learning to drive and seeing Mom's dinosaur stomp all over the East Coast (or the West!) and so many things. And now I have a new one, obvi, which is meeting YOU, my twin sister, Ruby Starling!!!

And, I guess, to meet my birth mom. Delilah Starling. Her. The one who gave me away, even though I was sick.

Even though I needed a mom more than anything. Even though I was probably going to die, but didn't.

I don't know how to stop being so angry, Ruby. I just don't know if I know how to do it. I want to. I really want to. I'm TRYING to. But it isn't working.

I'm still mad.

Do you understand?

Please please please say that you do.

Love,

Ruth

FROM: **Jedgar Allen Johnston** JedgarAllenPoe@yahoo.com

TO: **Ruth Quayle** iamruthquayle@gmail.com

I've been thinking about the script, and maybe we could use, like, *every* language in the world and then it could be a UNIVERSAL movie. One that speaks to everyone and basically means everything. Has anyone done that before? It could practically be a metaphor for *life*. For everything. Ever. But that sounds like a *lot* for five minutes or less. Maybe I'll stick to the animated line drawings and the SHORCAs in the toilet, superimposed over the drawings. The blue water works like blue screen in movies so it's kind of perfect, because I've figured out a way to make it seem like the clay

SHORCAs are eating the paper people. It's amazing, I think. I'm putting a post on the Internet about the Jedgar Method. Do you think I could, like, patent it? And get rich? I'm just kind of thinking out loud. But not out loud — thinking while I type. What's up? Where are you?

FROM: **Ruth Quayle** iamruthquayle@gmail.com

TO: **Jedgar Allen Johnston** JedgarAllenPoe@yahoo.com

What? I can't talk about *SHORCA!* I am much too busy crying. Please leave me alone.

FROM: **Jedgar Allen Johnston** JedgarAllenPoe@yahoo.com

TO: **Ruth Quayle** iamruthquayle@gmail.com

What? Why? Are you OK? Or are you joking? We have to talk about *SHORCA!*, seriously.

Mom said that if our movies had a double meaning, like if the story was a metaphor for something really cool, then they'd go viral. But I can't think of how to make *SHORCA!* also about something else. Plus, you know, that video of a cat on a Roomba didn't have two meanings. So actually, that's a terrible idea and explains why Mom is not a famous viral video maker.

Still, her comment made me want to not make *SHORCA!* at all. Because she's right, annoyingly, and it doesn't have any larger meaning. It's just shock value and cool special effects. Sometimes when I'm working on stuff like this, I start to think, what's the point? Does the world actually need another shock value/special effects short video? WHY? Shouldn't I be saving starving kids or something useful instead of wasting so much time on this?

Then I get pretty depressed.

But now we have this other thing that fell in our laps, which is your story about finding Ruby Starling on the Internet. So maybe we should make a documentary about you and her instead. I mean, it's pretty freaking amazing, and people *like* twin stuff. I found a whole bunch of it when I Googled. Some of it was completely bizarro, like this one pair of twins who were raised separately but both grew up to have the same job and to marry men named Bob. I guess that's not that much of a coincidence seeing as back in the 1960s, everyone was named Bob. But still, it's kind of freakishly cool.

I did some drawings of you finding Ruby — can you just look? It could be sort of like a comic book but with real talking and feelings and stuff like that, if you want. I had to do therapy after I lit that fire in fourth grade BY MISTAKE so I know what it is like, and making a movie about your experience would be better, therapeutically, for you. I think. I'm not, like, a therapy expert or anything. Anyway, I won't do it if you don't want me to but it's TOTALLY got an edge over a chomping shark/orca hybrid horror movie because it's, you know, *real*. It's your real, actual story. And that's pretty cool.

And it probably wouldn't need a double meaning to go viral.

NO WAY. I can't even believe you are asking me that! That's a terrible idea. Is this because you are still mad about the thing that we said we weren't ever going to talk about again? It's really unfair of you to do that when I'm in the midst of TURMOIL. Turmoil! EMOTIONAL TURMOIL, JEDGAR JOHNSTON! I totes know how celebs feel now when their so-called friends sell their stories to the tabloids, which is terrible. That's how they feel. Terrible.

You didn't even ask me why I was crying over here, alone on my island, which is what a real actual friend would have done instead of going on and on about double meanings found in movies about SHORCAs. What would

Buddha say about that? I'll ask Dad, but I'm guessing probably something like, "If you can't be a friend to your friend
when she is having a life crisis, then you probably are not
going to find peace in the sky and/or in drawing animated
movies about the tragedies in her life."

Actually, there is an actual real Buddha quote that fits,
which is, "The tongue, like a sharp knife, kills without
drawing blood." Which is a ridiculous quote, because of
course a knife that kills you draws blood, but what it means,
Jedgar, is that this whole thing about having a real mom and
a twin sister in England is killing me. Without blood.

Do you know what I mean?

FROM: Jedgar Allen Johnston JedgarAllenPoe@yahoo.com

TO: Ruth Quayle iamruthquayle@gmail.com

I did SO ask! I said, "Are you OK? What happened?"

And WHAT? Call me! Right now! So we can talk about
your REAL MOM?!?

Anyway, a lot of things don't have to happen for you to
know what it would be like. If a SHORCA chomped off my
leg, I'm guessing it would hurt. This is the same sort of thing,
if you think about it. That was my attempt at Buddhist wisdom. What do you think? Your dad would probably approve.

You do know that he's sort of not quite teaching you the point of Buddhism, right? Like the main parts? That calendar misses a lot of the big stuff. You can borrow my books about it if you want. It's totally interesting.

But Buddhism doesn't matter right now. I'm sorry that you're freaked out. I won't talk to you about *SHORCA!* or the Documentary of You until you want to, if you want to. If you don't, I'll just be over here, fending off my brothers AND WAITING FOR YOU TO CALL. (Should I come over?) The bros are doing something really alarming with Mentos and Diet Coke. Does Diet Coke stain? Because this is my favorite shirt and . . . oh, crap, I have to go. Diet Coke in the keyboard is probably not good.

FROM: **Ruth Quayle** iamruthquayle@gmail.com

TO: **Jedgar Allen Johnston** JedgarAllenPoe@yahoo.com

I'm sorry. I don't mean to take it out on you. I don't know why I am. I'm just pretty mad at EVERYONE right now! I can't explain! I am completely not on the Buddhist path! I'm off the path! Lost in the jungle! I am not "one with the path" or whatever, I've actually fallen into the river of rage and I'm drowning! Help! And I totes don't have time to read helpful Buddhist books about it either!

In other news, Mom is home. My actual mom, not the mom of my twin-sister-who-lives-in-England-who-obviously-gave-me-away.

I am going to talk to her. (MY mom, that is.)

RIGHT NOW!

OR IN A FEW MINUTES!

You know when you try not to think about a thing because you are thinking about something else, the thing comes to you anyway? So even though I am temporarily on a break from *SHORCA!* and any and all chomping, I just had an idea for an ending. How about it turns out that the SHORCA has a twin she did not know about and is not, in fact, mostly alone in the world after all? And THEN she obviously becomes much less short-tempered and apt to eat frolicking children and fishermen, and everyone lives happily ever after. Because by finding another SHORCA, she finds herself. What do you think?

There is your double meaning, Jedgar Johnston! It was right there, in front of our faces, all along. That's what it was about the whole time. Just not being alone.

I do not suggest that you introduce the SHORCA to her real parents, a shark and an orca, who aren't poor students, after all, but rather perfectly capable artists who live in England and just chose to leave her behind. That would be entirely too much for a three-minute film.

And now I'm crying again. I don't know why I keep crying. You would not want to be around me right now.

EMOTIONAL TURMOIL is really a lot worse than it sounds. And better. Both.

P.S. Jedgar Johnston, I am not joking when I say I DO NOT want you to take my pain and make it into a movie. I don't think you get how serious I am because sometimes I'm only half serious and half joking, so I have made the following contract. Please sign it. Thank you very much. I still love you and stuff, in a BFF way, I'm just confused, so if you think I'm mad, you're probably right, but if you think I'm not mad anymore, then you're right about that too.

CONTRACT BETWEEN RUTH E. QUAYLE AND JEDGAR A. JOHNSTON

I, Jedgar Allen Johnston, do solemnly swear on my future grave that I will not use Ruth Elizabeth Quayle's life story as material for a documentary about what happens when you find your twin using FaceTrace and she lives in England with your real mother, who gave you up when you were born, even though she kept your twin, for reasons that have not yet been explained, no matter how fascinating that documentary sounds and how many millions of people would want to watch it on the Internet. I further promise to finish making SHORCA! *with or without the sculpted SHORCAs made by Ruth Elizabeth Quayle, but giving Ruth Elizabeth Quayle credit for her IDEAS. Even FURTHER, I promise to be a good friend to Ruth Elizabeth Quayle at all times no matter what, even if my feelings change about her romantically, which I promise to never mention again and I will stop acting weird about RIGHT AWAY.*

Signed,

_____

JEDGAR A. JOHNSTON
(sign your name here)(if you want)

FROM: Fiona fififionafifi@aol.co.uk

TO: Ruby Starling starling_girl@mail.com

Ruby, we're all really really worried about you. We spent half of Hawkster's do just sitting in the garden and talking about you and your possible American twin situation. (Me and Chlophie, that is. The boys were watching the football. And the other girls were pretending to be really keen on football too, so the boys would think they were cool. But the boys didn't notice! Dead boring, really.) Look, it's just a lot to take in and it can't be any good that you are there alone, thinking that your nan is haunting your mum's old studio. We can't have you going bonkers. So you should come and stay with me and I'll help you with all of it. Mum and Dad say of course you can stay. So get your things and come to mine! The Mole is just banging on about how he's going out the door to go on some sort of horrid computer course in the Cotswolds. Apparently he's leaving first thing tomorrow. So he won't even be here, staring at you grimly over his Weetabix and wiping his drippy nose on his sleeve. Honestly, I don't know why he's so disgusting and what exactly he smells of.

FROM: Ruby Starling starling_girl@mail.com

TO: Fiona fififionafifi@aol.co.uk

Gosh, that's lovely of you. Am sure Mum won't mind, but I'll message her right now. Will call you as soon as I can! (I can't just come without clearing it with her first! What if she came home and I wasn't here? She'd go mental. So I'll come in the morning, OK?)

PS — Are you sure the Mole is going away? It's just that he is a bit annoying sometimes with his hangdog staring, like you always say. What do you mean, exactly, about his smell? He smells like soap. Just like you do. Not that I've been sniffing him.

Mum,

Can you please stop and pick up some milk on the way home from work? I'm going to go stay with Fi for a few days. Is that OK? I don't much like being alone at home all the time, is the thing, especially during the vac, and I understand that time is all meaningless and silly when you're working, but the thing is that it does get awfully dark and the house is so bumpy and loud. Not that I'm afraid, nothing like that. I'm fine, really. But I'll be here still tonight and I'll go to Fi's in the morning. There is something else too. Because . . .

It's just that, do you think that you and I could have a chat later? If you're home early enough. It's not anything important, so don't get worried, except it is a little bit important, Mum. I really do need to talk to you.

I think you should also get chocolate. Maybe we can watch *EastEnders* and think about Nan, just like we used to, only we didn't used to have to think about her, because she was there in her awful chair, shouting at us to be quiet so she could hear her stories. Can you set your phone to go off at half five so you make it on time? Just in case you lose track again.

Love,

Ruby

Ruby, darling, I'll be ages still — working on the tricky bits, like the ears. (Oh, our wonky ears!) I can't possibly leave at half five or at all until this is done! It'll set all wrong. Can you get the milk and bread? Just cycle into town. Or walk! There is money in the jar, it should be enough. Stop in and say hi if you like. But we don't need milk and bread if you're off to Fi's. I'll just eat at the café, and Fi's mum makes those lovely meals for you when you're there, with proper organic things. I admire her so much for that. Have some tinned spag for tea, you used to love that when you were little. I'm sure I saw some in the cupboard.

Get some chocolate, or whatever you like, for a treat. See if they have any of those chocolate biscuits that Nan used to like with her tea. I've just thought of those. Probably Nan's way of saying hello from the Great Beyond, d'you think? Or maybe she just approves of your plan for some telly, which I'd love to do, but I just can't. I can't. I'm so overwhelmed with this work. It's for you, dar-ling. Dedicated to you properly on a little plaque. Just like everything.

Don't wait up, sweetheart. Have a lovely time with your

friends! We'll have a good long goss when I'm done with this project, OK?

By the way, a spotty-faced boy was watching me measure out some of the space earlier, where the statue will go, and just when I was getting a bit annoyed that he was there, he finally approached me. He said, 'Cor, that's lovely. Know a girl who looks just like that photo, like, over there, I do. Ruby. She's a looker'. There's a big photo by the site of what the statue's going to look like, of course. Anyway, darling, I think he might have a little crush. Awfully funny-looking, but you know sometimes funny-looking boys are far nicer in the long run than attractive boys. I gave him your email — was that OK? Don't be cross. He just looked so hopeless, I couldn't help it. It was quite romantic really. In a funny way, he reminded me of your dad. Not that your dad was ever spotty. He was always just perfect. Just the way he should have been. We still miss him, don't we? So much.

x
Mum

Dear Nan,

~~How are you? I am fine.~~

~~So, Nan, it's come to my attention that . . .~~

Nan. I know it's different being dead than being alive. I mean, you're dead and just a cobwebby spirit, spinning your colours across the sky. I bet you stretch all around, everywhere, all silken light, like a big prismy rainbow with no start or finish. I think you'd like that. But if it's different from that, if you can get together with people and chat and whatnot, d'you think you could track down my dad? Philippe? And maybe ask him what happened and why they gave Ruth away, and then *tell* me?

And, being dead and all, maybe it doesn't matter to you that much what is going on down here. But I hope it does. I hope you still care. Because, Nan, I am really upset. And I can't talk to Mum yet and I don't think Fi will really understand.

It's just that Ruth is right to be furious. I FEEL GUILTY. Like it's my fault! But it isn't, Nan! I was just a new baby! How did it happen? How could you have let Mum do that? I want to understand, Nan, in a way that has nothing to do with you haunting the stairwell and making upsetting noises in the fireplace and knocking over paintings. I need to understand in words! Properly!

I've barely seen Mum the last few days, just when she dashes past me in the hall to the bath so she can soak off some of the clay that seems to be all over her, mostly in her hair. I know you used to say, 'Oh, Ruby, just leave her alone, she'll be back to herself when it's done' when she got madly intense about her work and stopped noticing anything (or anyone) else. But I wish she'd see that I'm upset! What kind of terrible mum doesn't know when her daughter is going completely mad?

I am simply *shattered.* You must find SOME WAY to tell me what you know. I promise I won't be frightened, at least not too much.

I got the letter magnets. I don't mind Mum teasing me about them, if you can use them to spell things out. I put all the vowels on one side. It doesn't have to be proper spelling, Nan, just see what you can do.

Maybe if you could just answer this: Did Mum give Ruth away because she was *broken?* Would she do that? It's so cruel! The worst, worst thing! 'Here, take my defective baby and I'll keep the good one, doctor! Thanks very much, we'll just be off then'. I can't stop picturing it, like it's a film that's playing in my head and I can't shut it off.

I am gutted about all of this, Nan. Well and truly gutted, like a fish that's been hacked open and filleted at the fish market. It's like I can't even quite remember who I used to be, just plain old Ruby, with the scatty Mum, a good eye for fashion, fab friends, and a mad crush on Nate from STOP. I want to be *that* Ruby again. It was so much simpler. But I don't know how to get back to myself from here. It's like I'm in a labyrinth and I've forgotten whether it's left or right at the next turning and I'll be stuck in here forever.

I'm meant to be going to Fi's in the morning, so I ought to pack a bag, but I think I'll just lie on the floor of my wardrobe for a while with the lights off and my legs leaning up the wall. It might all make sense in the dark. Sometimes things do.

Soon I'll try to write back to Ruth, but all I can think of to say is that I'm sorry. Because I am. I'm just very, very sorry. It's unfair and wrong, is what it is, and there's no dressing that up like anything else.

Love,

Ruby

FROM: **Ruth Quayle** iamruthquayle@gmail.com

TO: **Ruby Starling** starling_girl@mail.com

Dear Ruby,

You don't have to read this if you don't want to, I mean, if you're thinking or whatnot. But it's like since the last time I wrote to you, all the feelings that I've had inside me for all these years have just become unbearable. Multitudes of thoughts! And I can't even write a poem about them, because there are too many of them. They are like a million fireflies that I can't put into a jar and also can't ignore, because they are bright and buzzing around my head.

Don't tell my dad, but I really needed some answers, so I snuck a look ahead in the page-a-day calendar, to see if Buddha had anything that might help. And I found this: "Hatred does not cease through hatred at any time. Hatred ceases through love. This is an unalterable law." It seems to me that Buddha doesn't say very much that isn't obvious, but also — at the same time — completely impossible. Yes, I know that hating your mom isn't going to do any of us any good. It's not going to change what has happened or make what happens in the future better or make me feel good right now. But it's there, right there, next to Ashley Mary Jane's heart, in my chest, like a small black box that's somehow stuck in me. And Buddha isn't telling me how to dislodge the box! I don't know how.

Then I read this one, "Do not dwell in the past, do not dream of the future, concentrate the mind on the present moment." So that's what I'm trying to do. I am concentrating very hard on this absolute exact second, and how my fingers are typing on the keyboard, and the letters are a bit lit up because it's dark in here, and I guess that happens automatically, but I've never noticed it before. And my dog Caleb is lying across my feet, and sleeping, and kind of huffing in his sleep, and his breath is terrible, like he's just eaten some kind of rodent that's been dead for a long while, but he's so cute that I don't want to move him. So that's this moment: crumbs on the keyboard, a smear on the screen, the smell of something awful, and my fingers are moving moving moving and typing this to you, Ruby Starling, my twin sister who lives in England.

I keep saying that part. My twin sister! Who lives in England! And then I breathe in and out when I say it, smelling Caleb's awful breath, but still saying it, and then it's like meditating, which I think Buddhists are very fond of. Dad likes to meditate before work every morning, which might sound silly — because Dad is often silly and it's hard to take much he says VERY seriously — but he does it for real. He sits cross-legged on the patterned carpet on the living room floor and he closes his eyes. And I stare at him and sometimes make faces, but he doesn't move or flinch or laugh at me. And when I watch him, it's for real like something is flowing out of him. I guess that's why I listen about all this stuff he says about Buddha, even though there is a small part of me that thinks, "What? What are you talking about, Dad? Why can't you glom on to a more normal religion? Why is there a golden Buddha in our front yard? Just WHY?"

But there he is, all relaxed and stuff, and then he gets up and brushes off his pants — Caleb sheds a lot — and goes off to work. What he does (heart surgery) is über-stressful. Obviously. And he says that meditating changes everything. And so does the calendar, with all its "You cannot travel the path until you have become the path itself."

I think what I mean is that I'm trying to be the path.

Except I don't feel like a path. I feel a lot more wishy-washy than I would imagine a nice, solid, packed-dirt path would feel. Maybe more like a river. A rushing river of feelings. Mixed-up, messy, sort of horrible feelings. And the trouble is with feelings is that when some of them get messed up, it's like it uncorks all these other messy feelings and now I am completely and entirely AWASH WITH FEELINGS.

Such as: I've never had a real best friend and I think you are going to be my actual, lifelong best friend, being my twin and all. And that makes me happy. But also, it makes me feel like I shouldn't lie to you, and I lied before when I said I wasn't scared of dying.

I am totes scared of dying.

Part of the reason why I never really have close real friends (except Jedgar, obvi) is — according to my mom — because I've *always* thought I was going to die soon, even though I know I'm *probably* not. Ashley Mary Jane's heart is almost as good as my own now. It's all grown into my body, just like it's been there all along. Almost. I mean, I take bunches of pills that keep my blood from getting all stopped up in it, like a big scab, and things to make my body not suddenly reject it. Did you know that all the cells in your body renew every seven years? It's been more than seven years, so I don't even have any of AMJ's cells left anymore! The heart is all mine! 100% Ruth Elizabeth Quayle!

But I am still super, extra, always scared.

I know it's lame and I would never tell anyone because it seems important that I be brave and not wimpy and annoying.

And anyway, Dad is an *amaaaaazing* heart surgeon, as I've mentioned (though it is illegal for him to operate on me, his own actual adopted daughter!), and he says that I'm just fine and will be just fine forever, because I'm a fighter, and so I believe him. Mostly! Or I try hard to believe him! Which is sort of the same!

That's what I have to believe, to keep going and not spend my whole life lying very still in my room, trying not to disturb my heart muscles.

So *anyway*, Mom says that I *subconsciously want to protect people* from being my friend, to spare them the grief if I die. I think this is complete and total 100% Oscar Mayer baloney, except the part that is *maybe* a little bit true, like maybe 2.3%. *Maybe* I picked Jedgar because even though he has a lot of *feelings* (i.e. crushes on me), he never ever ever cries and he isn't a girl, so we could never really be as utterly, totally close as BFFs who are both girls and can coo together hilariously about boys and makeup and shoes and fashion and all our truest, most embarrassing secrets, like girl BFFs do. At least, in novels.

Anyway, I just had to get that out.

I AM scared.

Sometimes.

And I want to tell you this: I am not mad at you. I'm really not. I'm glad she picked you. You seem really cool and I would have picked you too.

Also, late, late, late last night (earlier than now, but still late), I happened to be up getting a glass of water, not from the kitchen or from my own bathroom, but from the en suite bathroom beside my parents' room, and I accidentally got into their bathtub and waited there until they went to bed. I can't really tell you why I did this, except that I'd wanted to talk to Mom all evening, but every time I tried, I felt like Dad was kind of stopping me from bringing anything up. I thought to myself, "He is going to talk to her about everything after I go to bed and I won't hear the whole of it because they will only tell me the very few facts they think I should hear." So I decided to use the faucet in their bathroom.

It took a long time for them to even bring me up in conversation, which was kind of disappointing, because Dad had to tell seven stories about heart operations and then Mom had to emphatically discuss the fact that what her trip really taught her is that maybe all her research is just going to turn into a funny article on a website and maybe they should pack everything up and start a hobby farm in Wisconsin. (Oh, please, NO. I don't like goats.)

I was very uncomfortable and also was extremely thirsty, but I didn't want to alert them to my whereabouts by running the tap. Then the conversation got interesting-ish (ACTUAL TRANSCRIPT BELOW):

Dad: So Ruth has found a . . . *blah blah* . . . Internet . . . Don't overreact. I don't know but . . . really do look alike. . . . Think she's right . . . so I think we have to . . . twins.

Mom: WHAT? Is THAT why she is acting so strangely? WHY DIDN'T SHE TELL ME? Doesn't she trust me?

Dad: I guess there's a . . . I don't . . . I told her . . . And then . . . But I think it means . . .

Mom: You're going to have to . . . [*mumble mumble*] right to know. I mean, if . . . I guess it could . . . so we . . . find out. [*crying*] She says . . . adopted? But . . . how can that? What kind of mother . . . one baby? Unbelievable!

Dad: It's just . . . *blah blah blah* . . . and also . . . *blah blah blah* . . . up to her. It's not, it's not that she thinks we're not, it's that . . . Did you let the dog in?

Mom: But Ruth is going to . . . and she . . . she'll think . . . and then . . . .

Dad: Ruth is a thirteen-year-old girl! She has an imagination as big as a mouse! [Or maybe he said "house." Probably "house"! (I do have a big imagination, it's true.)]

Mom: She's twelve.

Dad: [*sighing*] She's ALMOST thirteen.

Mom: Why do you always round up? It's so annoying. You're making her grow up too fast!

Dad: [*mumble*]

Mom: You know, [*mumble*]. I can't keep [*mumble*]. It's not good for her heart.

Dad: Ruth is . . . [*mumble mumble*] Have you seen my [*mumble*]?

Mom: They said that they [*mumble mumble*] and it won't be long before they [*mumble*].

Dad: Oh, Gen. [My mom is named Gen.] Please stop crying. You're taking this all wrong. And where IS the dog?

Mom: Why do I always have to let the dog in? He's *your* dog.

Dad: Do you hear something in the bathroom? Is Caleb in the BATHROOM?

Mom: No! I didn't [*mumble-shout*] your dog in the bathroom!

Dad: I'm going! I'm just first going to . . . RUTH, WHY ARE YOU IN THE BATHTUB?

After I was sent to my room in shame and despair and quite sore from having crouched for so long in the tub, I pulled my huge box of photos out of my closet. Mom is always printing out her "good" photos, which means "every photo my mom takes because she thinks she is very good at taking photos, which she does constantly." I got a little weepy when I found the pictures of baby me with the tubes all over me in the hospital. I was soooooo teeny, like a wet, unfurry, newborn kitten and not like an actual person at all.

While I was looking at the pics, Mom came barging in without knocking, so I threw the pictures unceremoniously off the back edge of my bed. (I didn't want Mom to see them because they make her weep, and when Mom weeps, I feel like my whole body is being turned inside out and walloped with a stick. It's too sad.) I pretended that I'd simply fallen asleep with my head akimbo. I think it worked. She straightened my neck and checked my pulse and tucked me in, like she does. Then she left the room.

I just wasn't ready to talk to her yet. I couldn't stand to be making her sad. Then I lay awake, then I sat up, then I started writing this to you. And thinking. And then writing some more. And thinking. And the house got very quiet, and even Caleb stopped snoring and galumphed off my feet and wandered down to his own bed (read: the couch), and now, you aren't going to believe this, but it's MORNING. I've been up all night! The sun is just creeping up outside my window and the birds are ker-chirping like they are the official alarm clocks of everyone in the land. STOP CHIRPING, BIRDS.

Ruby, I'm sorry that I keep writing and writing and writing. It's just all so *important*. I can't seem to stop.

Love,

Ruth

P.S. I've attached a photo of me when I was a tiny baby with wires and tubes and big eyes like saucers and the cutest tuft of hair ever! Just in case it seems like something you might want to see.

FROM: **Angus Da Man** (angus_da_man@aol.co.uk)

TO: **Ruby Starling** (starling_girl@mail.com)

Hiya. Got your e from your mum. She's right talented, innit? Anyway, was wondering if you wanted to go out. Hang about or whatever. Won't be crushed or anything if you don't want to. OK then, I'm off. Angus.

PS — I work at the chip shop, in case you didn't know. But sure you know me, everyone does, yeah?

FROM: **Ruby Starling** (starling_girl@mail.com)

TO: **Angus Da Man** (angus_da_man@aol.co.uk)

Is this a joke? Get stuffed! I'm 12. What are you, 16? I don't know what Mum was thinking, she must've thought you were much younger than you are. Honestly, don't be such a creep. I'm not into you.

You're not going to believe this, but I've had an e from the SPOTTY CHIP SHOP BOY. His name's Angus, don't you know, and he expects everyone to know it. Fancies himself, I think. For goodness' sake, Mum has terrible taste in boys, even when they aren't for her. He sent the most dreadful message about how he doesn't really fancy me, so who cares if I want to hang out with him or not? Well, I DON'T.

There's nothing I care less about right now than BOYS anyway. I haven't even been thinking about Nate very much, which is really rare. I'm not able to think of anything but Ruth! I've found out loads more things, such as: She was born with a bad heart. They expected she'd die, but she had a transplant and she survived. And it really looks like Mum gave her away because of her manky heart. There can't be any other reason a person would have twin babies in America and then just leave one of them there. It's impossible to get my head round! A person who would do a thing like that is an awful person. And she's my own mum! I never thought she was perfect or even very good at being a mum, but she's my only mum.

My head's bursting. I think Ruth might be a hippie, like those women we met from Camden last year. She talks a lot about Buddha. I wonder if she wears sandals and those skirts with the mirrors on? Those are naff. But that doesn't even matter. What matters is that I have a twin in AMERICA who my mum gave away and no one can give me any answers and I don't know what to DO or what to say to Ruth or what to say to Mum or really anything!

The e from the Chip Shop Boy was the last straw. I was just going to come to yours, Fi, but I called you and the Mole answered so I just hung up quickly before he could tell it was me. Thought you said he was going away this morning! I can't come and stay if he's there! Ugh.

Ruby

Gosh, Rube Rube, that's all super intense! It's like a film, yeah? So we're sure it will have a happy ending, though we can't think what. We want to race right over and give you hugs and fix your hair up until you feel better about things, not that it would change anything, just that it would cheer you up. But we can't because SOPHIE is going to see a film with Hawkster. Like a proper date!

And this is where it gets a bit of a funny story, Ru! It's like, when she told me, I was all, 'What am I meant to do? Stay home and be soooo lonely and cut my fringe too short and then weep from the ugliness? No! NOOOO'! I had to go with them, I just had to, so *I* asked the Spotty Chip Shop Boy.

ANGUS.

And he said, 'Yeah, all right then'.

But that was before I knew he was dashing off lurve notes to YOU! And now he's TWO-TIMING? What a prat! He's the worst! I'm furious! Like really really furious! And we haven't even gone out yet! I think I should dump him! Right now!

Should I still go, do you think?

Oh, Sophie wants to know if she should wear a skirt or would that look like she cared, because she doesn't, so maybe she'll just go in her jeans. Can't think why Soph cares what she wears. She should wear a bin bag, far as I'm concerned. And act like she doesn't even realllllly like him at all, 'cause she doesn't! It's just that he's popular, isn't he? And he looks fit from very far away?

Are you cross about Angus? It's just that if he fancies you then he's sort of yours, yeah? Like you have dibs on Nate. This can't come between us being mates, it isn't worth it. It makes me feel wistful! Just thinking about how looooong ago, we used to not care about boys. Oh, got to go! Have got to curl my hair before we meet the boys! We'll be thinking about you loads though, about your mum and all that, and . . . I AM TELLING HER, SOPHIE, GET OFF.

Sophie says that it isn't as bad as all that, and everything will work out, and we love you, smooches and hugs and *besos*! Talk soon. Wish us luck! Byeeeeeee.

FROM: **Ruby Starling** starling_girl@mail.com

TO: **Chlophie!!!** chlophie@hotmail.co.uk

You're going to a film with HAWKSTER and *Angus*? They're total rubbish, both of them! I'm attaching the e that Angus sent me. You deserve *way* better! Hold out for someone nice! Someone like Nate. Why d'you want boyfriends anyway? I'd rather eat my own sick than see a film with those yobs.

PS — Thanks, about the other stuff. There must be an explanation and I'm sure Mum will tell me everything soon.

The Mole's gone now! I swear! He just had to come back because he forgot his giant, dorky headphones so he can listen to his music on the train and look like a complete wally while he's doing it. COME ROUND.

From The Mole to Ruby (handwritten on lined paper)

Hey Ruby,

Thing is that I know it's off. The way you call me the Mole and everything gives it away. You know, I know how it is. But it's like I can't help how I feel. I guess I wanted to say that. It's like a magnet. Like we fit or something. That felt stupid to write. You're probably laughing.

You should throw this away. Don't let Fi see it. She'd laugh so hard, she'd probably drop dead. (Did you know there are ten deaths listed on Wikipedia under "died laughing"? Truth.) Adding Fi to the list wouldn't be so bad. (That's a joke.)

Maybe you could leave me a note in my room if you want. Not if you don't. I get it. You don't have to.

See you around.

Ed

Dear Ms. Ruth Quayle:

To whom it may concern:

I have signed the contract.

Sincerely,

Jedgar A. Johnston

Ruth, are you being weirder than you usually are? I can't tell sometimes if you're being funny or not, like you're making fun of me but I'm not supposed to get it. But I do get it, so it's either not funny or just mean. I wish I could unwind time and go back to Drop Mac and un-ask you what I asked you, because it wasn't worth this awkwardness, if that's what this is. And really, I am not taking advantage of your story, it's just that it's super awesome and I can totally see how to do it so you'll think it's awesome too. I know you're all confused about it and I guess that because you're a girl and stuff, you are feeling a lot of things about having a twin and a real mom, but if you think about it, none of it changes YOU. You are still you. This is all stuff that is happening around you, but not TO you, not really. Do you get what I mean? It's like even if this didn't happen, you'd still be exactly like you've always been. But now you know your real mom and that you have a sister, it's like a bonus. Like extra stuff. It doesn't take away anything from you, is what I sort of mean.

If I make the film, it would be like a comic book, except animated. So it's not really YOU, it's just a drawing of you, so that other people can see it and go, "Wow, that's a totally amazing thing that happened!" and they can see how you are still you. I think that's the part that's the most important, you still being you. I feel like maybe you don't think you are, and that's why you're acting all crazy and weird.

But I won't do it if you don't want me to, but I want to, which I'm saying just so we're clear and later you don't go, "What? I didn't know you wanted to do that!"

Anyway, whatever. You're still you and you're still my best friend and all that.

Mea culpa,

Jedgar

Mom,

I'm sorry about spa day. I wrecked it! It's my fault. As Jedgar would say, "MEA CULPA," which is an actual thing that he's taken to saying all the time, like he's an elderly Latin scholar and not a 13-year-old boy. (You were absolutely right about me needing more girl friends and I'm working hard at finding more, because ever since the Incident, Jedgar has been weird. Not FRAUGHT, but definitely different.)

Anyway, here is what I need to say to you, Mom:

I'm sorry! I'm sorry! I'M SUPER EXTRA SORRY!

OK?

Mom?

You know, when I asked you why I have a twin sister named Ruby Starling who lives in England, I *totes* completely didn't know that you'd run out of the spa with your nails half done and the Korean lady chasing you down the street, shouting.

That was weird, Mom. Even for you. (But also sort of awesome. All that running you've been doing when you travel is paying off! You're super fast.)

Are you mad? I don't really get it, whether you are mad or sad or if you've actually gone completely crazy and I should be calling 911. (That last part was a joke. I know you are not crazy.) I guess I just thought that you understood that this wasn't about finding my birth mother, but actually just about "GADZOOKS! I HAVE A TWIN!" It's definitely not that I want to trade you in. It is so so so so so not that.

You know that I've always said I don't care about my birth mother, and that's a lie, I do care. But not in a good way. Like I'm mad at her, Mom. I'm really mad. But I'm trying to understand what Dad's been teaching me about being angry and about how I shouldn't be angry. I know he wasn't talking about my birth mom, he just meant in general that anger is a waste of energy, and I get that. So I'm trying not to be angry with Delilah Starling. I am trying not to hate her.

I Googled her this morning.

Now I know what she looks like, and seriously, Mom, that's all I wanted to know, and now I do. I know she has long red hair and she paints stuff and sculpts stuff and sometimes builds crazy-looking stuff out of metal, and that stuff is usually . . . me. Which is weird. It is the weirdest. She's basically spent all this time making me out of clay and paint and paper clips and whatever! Everything! Like my image is interesting or useful to her big fantastic OMG artistic career, but the actual ME isn't/wasn't good enough for her?

Mom, I hate her. I really do. Don't tell Dad. It's like basically the opposite of everything he's trying to teach me about Buddha and inner peace and all that stuff that's super important to him! I know it! But it's true.

I'm not even sure I ever want to meet her. I guess I'm scared. She gave me away and I can't rewrite that in my head to make it a good story, or even to make it OK. It just sucks. She obviously didn't want me, she wanted Ruby. And she got her. So why should she even *get* to meet me? It's much more super complicated than I ever thought it would be when I first started thinking about being adopted and how one day, maybe on the bus, or in line for Space Mountain, I might bump into the woman who was my actual mother, and then I'd be able to look at her with great disdain and she would see how great I was and she would regret giving me away because I turned out to be so awesome. I was sort of thinking it would happen more when I was a grown-up, and not exactly NOW.

I'm not ready.

And I am not awesome.

And I'm weirdly so sad, it's like the sad is squashing out all the other feelings. I'm so full of sad that I only have a bit of room left for MAD, but even that little bit of mad is making me sick. Dad's right!

Mom, it's all messing up what's really important, which is that I really really really want to meet Ruby. SHE IS MY TWIN. The very same set of cells! But with an accent! And good fashion sense! So of course I want to meet *her*, Mom. OF COURSE I DO.

So would you, if you were me. Right?

Dad told me not to talk to you about it because it would

be upsetting, but it's not like you to get upset about this stuff. I don't want you to feel terrible, but I want you to want ME to not feel terrible too. And I DO feel terrible! The worst! And Dad's mad at me because he says I promised not to talk to you about it until you had a chance to figure out how you felt, but I didn't know how long that would be! I didn't know when it would be OK! And now, well, I've wrecked everything, I guess.

But Mom, even if you are upset, I have to ask you something. You said we could plan our trip this summer, and I need to see Ruby, for real. I need to. I really really really really need to. Can we please go to England? I know you were probably thinking Lake Wanabasco or possibly even Disneyland, but . . .

This is bigger than anything that's ever happened to me, like EVER. You know how you felt when you found out the Luffy cells might work? It's like that! But different. It's more personal. Mom, I never would have looked for my biological mom. Not on purpose. I love you! *You're* my mom! But she's my SISTER. I have to meet her, Mom.

I just chipped all of my nails typing this out. How does anyone have painted nails for more than five minutes? I don't understand nail polish. But there's lots of things I don't understand. Like boys and physics and Buddhism and why I'm so different from everyone else.

Mom, are you crying in your room? Because you are freaking me out. If you don't come out, I'm going to call

Dad. Or better yet, send Caleb *in*. And I can't be responsible if he rolls on your clean laundry.

Love you more than jumping into the lake from the dock,

Ruth

P.S. Please be OK.

P.P.S. I'm sorry.

FROM: **Gen Quayle** `Gen@usdinolab.org`

TO: **Ruth Quayle** `iamruthquayle@gmail.com`

Honey, I am *fine*. I am OK. It's just it was a shock. Hearing it from you, even when I'd already heard it from Dad.

I'm acting oddly, I know! You must be worried. But don't worry. There are some things happening at work, you know, about the Luffster. We should stop calling him that. We should call him the dinosaur. We should just say that, from now on. Because you shouldn't get attached to things that aren't real, do you know what I mean? But that's nothing to worry about, not for you!

I think I'm a little bit in shock about the twin in England. It's not something I was expecting! Life's funny like that, right? About what you expect and then about what actually happens. I could never have guessed this. Not in a million years. But, Ruth, I do think I knew that you'd go looking for your biological family one day. And then "one day" just snuck up on me.

I know you're mad at her, and I know you have to figure out your own path here. Dad gave me a great quote this morning: "The foot feels the foot when it feels the ground." You know I think his Buddhism-day-by-day thing is pretty ridiculous and that science doesn't leave much room for religion, but in a way, "The foot feels the foot when it feels the ground" is how I feel about all of this. By which I mean, I didn't know that this was going to happen. I just *thought* I knew what I'd feel. But now it's all hitting the ground, and now I know how the foot feels. I'm sure I'm butchering what Buddha actually meant, but I think you know what I mean.

You might feel like you're different from everyone, but you aren't. You're not all that different from me, Ruth. That's why I've always felt you were made to be my daughter. It was meant to happen, all of it.

Unexpected. There's so many unexpected things, Ruth! I guess if I teach you anything, as your mom, I hope I teach you about how things happen that are unexpected. I hope I teach you how to cope.

Plus, I haven't been sleeping. I can never sleep when I'm traveling! Insomnia is the worst. I'm going to take some melatonin and get some rest! I'll feel better after I've slept. Listen, Daddy wants to come to the park with you to watch you skateboarding and then have a nice dinner of baked-fried chicken at the beach. (I know it's not the same as fried-fried, but it's much healthier! It's in the fridge.) It will be fun, and Caleb and I will just have a long, long nap, and then everything will be fine.

And thanks so much for explaining to Ms. Kim about the situation. I don't know what you said, but she wouldn't let me pay, and she's given us a ham. It's in the fridge, but don't eat it. I'll make hamaroni for your dad's birthday next week. You know he loves it because he loves everything that has hardly any nutritional value.

Goodness, this melatonin is working! Yawn!

Love you more than squid ink pasta,

Mom

FROM: **Ruth Quayle**   iamruthquayle@gmail.com

TO: **David Quayle**   docdaddave@gmail.com

Dad? I can't have a picnic with you at Drop Mac, I'm going to Jedgar's house. We're just making SHORCAs because he's agreed to do *SHORCA!* in addition to a very, very small, insignificant documentary that no one will watch about my tragic story.

I know what you're thinking, which is, "WHAT? RUTH, WHY WOULD YOU LET JEDGAR MAKE A

DOCUMENTARY ABOUT FINDING YOUR TWIN ON THE INTERNET WHEN WE ARE STILL TRYING TO COPE AS A FAMILY WITH THIS NEWS?" And you are right to massively overreact! Because I did too! At first!

Then I changed my mind because of how things sometimes make more sense when you see them in a different way. But mostly you never can. You can only ever know what you were thinking, yourself, when stuff happens. EXCEPT if someone else tells the story, THEN you can see it from a totes different perspective! I imagine this is how Luna the killer whale felt when she saw the film *Killer Whale*. (Whales are very intelligent, you know, which is why *SHORCA!* was so brilliant in the first place, because it's about a terrifying killer shark who is also really, really smart, which makes her scarier, amirite?)

I think that when I see the whole story about me and Ruby in Jedgar's way, then I'll be all, "LOOK AT MY TWIN! THIS STORY IS AWESOME!" and not so much "I AM FEELING A LOT OF PANIC AND I DON'T KNOW WHY." I hope, anyway.

xoxo,
Ruth

Ruth,

Will you meet me at the park if we get McDonald's instead? DO NOT TELL YOUR MOM. I'll be there at 5. Be there or be a cube. (That's a joke, I know it's "square.")

    Daddy

DAD. Not Daddy. See you later, alligator. Get me a cheeseburger and a chocolate shake, OK? Please?

I am in Jedgar's bathtub right now, hiding behind the shower curtain. It would be funnier if his mom wasn't flipping out. If you don't hear from me in an hour, send help!

I'm kidding, I'll be fine. She's mad at the boys, not at me. Well, mostly because she doesn't know that I'm here.

Hey, so, I know you're probably mad, but I'm apologizing for my mom. She was super mean to you and that wasn't OK. It's not your fault about the towels, you were just trying to help. Besides, she's being unreasonable. How could we know that SHORCAs would block the toilet like that? I would have told her all this, but I was in my room trying to stop my idiot brothers from suffocating me with a pillow.

I think I have enough footage now anyway, and all I have left to work on is the drawings. So we agree that it's now going to be basically silent, except for the words in the bubbles above their heads like "HELP!" and *"AU SEC-OURS!"* and *"¡AYUDARME!"* and stuff. Then we'll just do a voice-over about the facts about SHORCAs, like how there is only one left in the world and she's lonely and misunderstood, because even though she's friends with both sharks AND orcas, she doesn't fit in with either group, and that's why she eats people. Well, that, and because she's hungry. Can you figure out how to put all that into a three-minute script, or are you totally too mad?

I have to go. Mom is turning purple and shouting again. Apparently I'm not allowed to use the computer until I've cleaned the carpet in the hallway. I didn't know toilets could even flood that far. I might die from the stench. If I do, I guess this is good-bye. *Au revoir. Adiós.*

J.

P.S. Why was my laptop in the bathtub? I guess that was good, because it didn't get wet when the toilet exploded, since the shower curtain was closed. But weird. I'm just glad no one took a shower.

FROM: **Ruby Starling** starling_girl@mail.com

TO: **Ruth Quayle** iamruthquayle@gmail.com

Dear Ruth,

I'm staying at my best friend Fi's. It's a madhouse here, even though it's just Fi and her mum and dad. (Her brother, the Mole, is away. Thank goodness.) He left me the most embarrassing note under my pillow! I can't tell Fi. She'd be angry. I don't know what to do so I'm going to pretend it fell between the pillow and the headboard, so I couldn't have seen it. Then he won't expect an answer.

When they talk to each other round here, they all talk at the same time instead of waiting for the first person to finish. Then they get louder and louder and louder and no one is listening and everyone is talking. Eventually I just gave up trying to have a conversation and snuck up to Fi's room to write to you. It's a bit like a room you would have picked out when you were little, with lots of purple and a canopy bed. I love it, but I'd never tell Fi. She thinks it's awful. Mum was never very into things like that, proper girly things. She said the light in my room was fantastic. And it is, really. But then she painted it really pale blue. It gives me migraines when the sun's out, because somehow the blue turns bright white, like snow. Maybe that's why I like the wardrobe so much.

The thing is, what I want to say, is that I'm sorry that Mum is . . . awful. She is awful, isn't she? She must be if she gave you away. I don't know why she did what she did, but it's rubbish. Whatever her reason is! It must be! But she isn't a bad person, she just sometimes gets easily overwhelmed. It's because of her art, I think. I'd say it was because Dad died, but I don't think that's true, I think it's just how she is. She's always half lost in whatever she's working on! I know that sounds like an excuse to make it seem OK, but it's true.

If Nan were here, she'd tell you. She always said that Mum was mad as a bag of ferrets when she had something on the go. She has something on the go all the time now, especially since Nan went. When she doesn't, she's either crying about Nan or pretending to be normal and asking me about boys and things and then not listening to my answers. (She thinks I fancy this awful boy, Angus, who works at the chip shop. And I let her think that, because it's easier than explaining that I'm in love with a pop star — Nate, from

STOP. It sounds silly when I say it out loud. Embarrassing, really. Even though I know that it's real. But you don't care about that right now, I know you don't. I know your feelings are all jumbled up. Just like mine. Only mine are a bit different, because I feel like it was my fault that she did it. I just don't know how. Or why.)

I'm sorry, Ruth. I wish Nan were here. You'd love her. And she'd know exactly the right thing to say. Right now, 'sorry' is pretty much all I've got. Again and again and times a million. Sorry.

Love,
Ruby

FROM: **Ruby Starling** starling_girl@mail.com

TO: **Delilah Starling** theartistdelilah@yahoo.co.uk

Mum, I'm at Fi's now, just reminding you.

We really really really need to talk. Mum, it's important. You said that I can always talk to you about important things. And I've never had anything. But now I do.

Darling! I've been thinking about it since your first message and I feel terrible! Why didn't you tell me you were nervous about being home alone? I should never have left you! I'm a poor excuse for a mum, aren't I? I'd have got you an alarm system or a guard dog or both if I'd known. Glad you're tucked up at Fi's. Pop round tomorrow and see the sculpture. I think it's almost done.

And of course we can talk! Whenever you like! I've missed you, my girl. Let's have a good long talk when I'm done with this thing and get our lives all straightened out and back to normal. I'm thinking that we should sort the house and bung out Nan's old things. Nan would have wanted her useful bits and bobs going to charity. We'll give it all away! Then we'll feel better. About everything. About Nan, is what I mean. Then she'll be gone.

Love,

Mummy xo

Mum, I didn't mean you were a bad mum! But I really mean it, about needing to talk to you. It's important this time.

Love,

Ruby

PS — I always call you Mum now, you know. I haven't said 'Mummy' since I was six! I just mention it because it's funny that you call yourself Mummy, isn't it? When I just say Mum?

nopoppingballoons.tumblr.com

When a thing happens,
a bad thing,
Everyone is sorry.

Picture a tree, falling over.
Is it sorry?
Or is it just a thing that happens
sometimes
when there is a lot of rain and wind?

Blame the weather.
I do.
It takes what it wants
and either blows it skyward
or lets it fall
to the ground
to die
without anyone
ever really knowing
why it happened.
And no one ever
apologizes
to the tree.
Which is probably
just fine with the tree,
if you think about it.

What would Buddha do?
Be the tree,
be the ground the tree landed on,
be the wind that pushed it over,
or just be sorry?

Ruby to Nan

Dear Nan,

I am at Fi's. It's lovely here and noisy and messy. You'd hate it but I love it.

This isn't really a letter. Not a proper one. It's more like a postcard, because I'm writing it on the back of a self-defence leaflet that Fi's dad gave me. (He's really determined!) Anyway, I feel like if I don't write to you a lot, then you'll be completely gone. And with Mum talking about getting rid of your things, I feel like you're fading away. Just now, I was trying to picture you sitting at the kitchen table, giving Mum a lecture about proper budgeting, and I couldn't picture your face! I couldn't remember it! Then I felt like I couldn't breathe.

And you haven't even once moved any of the letters on the fridge, Nan. So maybe the thing with the art was just a coincidence after all. But even if it was, it's true, so there.

Anyway, Fi just came in and crashed down on the bed with her arms flung over her face and said, 'They've completely lost it, Ruby. They've hired a caravan and they say that they're taking me on a holiday. I don't want to go'! So I said, 'It'll be lovely, I never get to go anywhere that's just for fun'. Then she stopped complaining because she felt sorry for me because she knows I'm right, Mum being so busy all the time. We only go on holiday if there's some sort of lecture she's making me go to with her.

Nan, can you see my laptop screen? Ruth e'd me a pic of her as a baby and you can see her scar. I can't stop looking at it. It's like a zipper all down her back, like she had wings once and they were just zipped off. Or maybe it's a place where wings could be zipped on, if she needs them. If you believe in angels and that sort of thing, which I don't. Not really.

I just want to sit down and have tea with you and tell you everything about Ruth, so I can sort out how I'm feeling. And I know this bit is silly, but I have to tell someone: Nate's started dating Star Howell, the *model-slash-actress-slash-girl-everyone-wants-to-be*, and I feel really betrayed. She's seriously beautiful. And now she has Nate too! It's as though I made it happen by not reading his blog every day. Ruth's distracted me, so it's almost like it's her fault. Am I going mad? Because I know that's completely barmy, it's just how I feel.

xo,

Ruby

RUBY,

STOP!

You can't be sorry!

I mean, you can! Obviously! You can do whatever you want!

But it's OK. You don't have to say it.

I just want US to be normal. I don't want it to be all you saying sorry and me saying it's OK, and you saying sorry and me saying it's OK, and you saying sorry and me saying it's OK. It isn't OK, but it isn't for you to be sorry about. It's not your fault. YOU WERE A BABY! It's sort of your mom's fault and I have to figure out, in my head, how to forgive her for that. But I'm not mad at you.

Please write me again, but about something else other than your sorry-ness, such as a list of seven things you did today or five worst foods or Things You Want To Do Before You Die or anything. Just not SORRY. Do not be sorry.

I was thinking, if we'd been kids together, you'd know all the weird stuff about me, like I sometimes tied my shoe-laces to my desk so I couldn't float away during class and/or it would make it harder for kidnappers to snatch me. And I'd know that you liked . . . something. Whatever you liked!

We need to know these things! So maybe if we can't answer the questions of WHY HOW WHAT and WHEN your mom did what she did, we can talk. Just talk. About random stuff. About everything. About anything.

I'm going to start.

How's the weather? I don't care about the weather so much, but maybe a little, because we are having a heat wave and my sweaty legs have glued me to this chair that I'm sitting on, and when I stand up, I'll have that weird sticky-ripping feeling when I try to peel my skin from the plastic. Also, my mom might be losing her job. I just stuck that there at the end so I don't have to talk about it. (She works super hard! It's so unfair! But I am in the moment! Stuck to the chair! Sweaty! Typing!) Dad says the change in the weather is probably good because people will start to figure out that global warming sucks and they will stop buying such giant cars. Dad thinks SUVs are the worst thing ever invented by mankind and represent all that is wrong with the world. Well, SUVs and the Internet. He might be right! Except not about the Internet, which is basically my favorite thing in the world. And I sort of wonder about him thinking about the repercussions of stuff like big vehicles if he's being Buddhist and staying in the moment. Because hey, life is totes suffering, and maybe the suffering comes in the form of large ugly cars and global warming and having your skin stuck horribly to the chair you are sitting on.

But that's not even what I want to talk about! I mostly want to know if we're the same, like in all the stuff I read about twins online, where they are both fans of wasabi and enjoy handstands and the electric guitar. Or if we are opposites, which could happen, and would maybe be even MORE interesting!

We should be specific and tell each other *specific* things. For example, I will tell you specifically that yesterday Jedgar and I were flushing SHORCAs down his toilet — for filming, not just for fun, of course — and the toilet got clogged. Can you believe it? Anyway, it was hilarious, except for the flood, and I swear I didn't know those were his mom's good towels. I just thought they never used them, so they'd be a good choice for the cleanup. I had to do it all because they'd all been sent to their rooms, Jedgar and his brothers, while I hid in the bathtub and pretended to not be there. I thought it would be HEROIC of me to do the cleaning! Then his mom wouldn't be mad! Well, my bad.

Anyway, Jedgar's mom called Tink Aaron-Martin's dad and he fixed it. He's nice, and so is Tink! I probably haven't mentioned her, but she's part of my Project To Have More Girl Friends Who Aren't Jedgar (Who Isn't Even A Girl, Even Though It's Hard To Think Of Him As A Real Boy Either). So now I have you and *sort of* Tink. I hope I didn't get her in trouble, because I told her dad that she was getting pretty good at skateboarding, which I also happen to be amazing at, and he sort of laughed and said, "That's funny, because she's grounded and not allowed out of the house!" I feel terrible, but I can't email her because she has no Internet now either.

Life is such a perfidious disaster sometimes! "Perfidious" is Jedgar's new word for everything. He loves words. He's crazy about words. If words were people, he would for sure marry one, only he wouldn't be able to pick his favorite. It changes. Last week, it was "phlegmatic." Maybe he's working his way through the *P* section of the dictionary.

Can you tell me things? Just anything that comes into your head. It doesn't have to be about being twins because that can just be there, thrumming along in the background, like a very quiet flute that is only a bit ominous. I especially want to know why the Mole is stuffing letters under your pillow!

Here, I will start with a list of the top five most embarrassing things that I ever did:

1. I was getting on the bus to go on a field trip to the aviation museum last year and I tripped and fell onto the bus driver's lap. It was super awful because as soon as I got off his lap, he put the bus in gear and drove away. BUT my shoe had fallen off and out the door when I fell. And I didn't want to mention it. AWKWARD. So I took off my other shoe and I went on the field trip barefoot. And no one even *noticed*. Which actually is totes tragic when you think about it. I could have died

from exposure! Except it was only October and it was just coolish, not actually like I was strolling around barefoot on the frozen tundra.

2. Once, during science, I had to go up to the front of the class and work out a chemistry equation on the board. When I got there, I realized that everyone was laughing. Like seriously howling with laughter and dramatically clutching at their sides and shrieking. Someone (WES STROMSON-FUNK, who is the WORST BOY IN THE CLASS and possibly on the planet) had stuck a sign on my back that said "I LOVE REPTILES." Why is that even funny? What if I did love reptiles? I do love dinosaurs. But anyway, I turned bright red and my eyes watered. The teacher, Mr. Wall, was terrified of crying students, so he whisked me off to the nurse's office. She gave me an orange. (I do not like citrus fruit.) On the plus side, I never had to do the equation.

3. Our school went on an outing to cheer up old people at Christmas, because obviously a class of middle-school kids who are crazed from candy consumption can do nothing but make people happy and filled with the holiday spirit. We were each assigned an old person and we had to basically just be cheerful, which is easy for me because I am usually cheerful! But my old person just wanted to watch *The Price Is Right*. I sat beside her and told her some fun things about what I was going to buy

for Mom and Dad for Christmas (and the prices, as she kept shouting out "A DOLLAR NINETY-NINE, YOU IMBECILE!"). While I was talking, I was gesturing dramatically with my hands, and I knocked a glass of water off her bedside table, which her teeth were in, and they totes FLEW out the open window and down four stories to the ground below. Actually that's the worst thing I've ever done, and now I have a balled-up feeling of being a bad person, nestled right there in my stomach like a boulder. Why didn't I tell someone? Or go crawl around in the shrubbery to find the teeth? I hope she had another set of teeth. She probably never chewed again!

4. I can't write a fourth thing because I'm now too upset about number 3. I am a seriously awful person, and your mum was maybe right, after all, to leave me behind and take you back to England to live happily ever after. If you ask old Mrs. Schwartz, she would almost certainly agree.

Ruth

I am not dead.

I have birds in my head,

flapping their ideas,

taut and feathery,

rushing by,

right now,

not tomorrow,

but this second, now this one

and this one too.

There is Ruby Starling

across the sea,

and me, here,

and us the same

but different

and her with our mom

and me with my own mom

and our whole lives of blocks and books

and boys

and Band-Aids

and I miss being read to.

Did her (our) mom

read to her?

I want to shout

ELEPHANT

ZOO

TUNA
RAIN.

Nothing makes sense.
My head is too full of everything
like a balloon
lifting me up off the ground
and soon I'll float up and up
and be part of the sky and the clouds
until the balloon is popped
a bird dies
and I fall
down
again.

FROM: **Ruby Starling** starling_girl@mail.com

TO: **Ruth Quayle** iamruthquayle@gmail.com

Ruth,

I've just read your Tumblr and I think I know what you mean, about your head and floating upwards, that bit. I feel like that too. This is just a lot to take in.

All around me, everyone is going on like things are normal. But things aren't normal! I want to stand up on the table at Starbucks and shout that out loud! 'STOP BEING NORMAL! I HAVE A TWIN IN AMERICA'! Chlophie and Fi are being *really* kind and everything, but they still want to spend all their time talking about clothes and boys and the tarot and the calories in a mocha, and I sort of just want to scream at them, 'LOOK WHAT IS HAPPENING'!

But the thing is, nothing is happening.

But I am not the same!

You don't need to feel badly about the teeth. Old people don't usually eat food they have to chew anyway. My nan stopped wearing her teeth when she got sick, right before she died. Your Mrs Schwartz probably just kept them in a jar by her bed, just in case. That's what Nan did. 'Just in case the Queen pops in', she'd say, and then she'd laugh. Nan loved the Queen. When you turn 100 in England, the Queen writes you a letter, but Nan was only 62 when she died. She'd had fake teeth since she was really young because her family was poor and they never had money for proper dentists and things. Nan hated those teeth. You probably did Mrs Schwartz a favour by tossing hers out the window!

I don't like talking about Nan. When I do, it's like something inside me starts trembling and won't stop. I wish you'd met her. She was lovely. She was the best.

I love lists! I think we are the same, in that twin way. Here are my top ten secrets. DO NOT tell anyone. Not that you know anyone who knows me, but just in case.

1. I never tell anyone secrets, not Mum, not Nan, not even Fi. Because they are secrets! And I'm worried that people will laugh or think I'm mental or both. So that's a secret itself, don't you think? I pretend to tell secrets. Like I'll tell Fi that I love Nate (which isn't a secret, everyone knows it already), but I don't tell her that I sometimes spend a long time hoping for things like terrible disasters that only Nate and I will survive, and then it's like I write a whole novel about it in my head, where we end up holding hands by the sea somewhere, with the sun setting after the apocalypse. Really corny, I know. I feel mortified that I think about things like that, but I can't seem to stop, and I can't seem to like regular boys. They're all wazzocks, every last one.

2. I sometimes get up at night when I can't sleep. My room is so pale, it sometimes glows. It's a bit like sleeping in a surgical suite. Then I go into my wardrobe and sleep there on the floor. I have blankets and things there, so it's cosy.

3. I only feel good about myself when someone is telling me how amazing my clothes are. I know that's vanity and Nan would say that it was meaningless tosh, but it means a lot to me. Mostly I buy all my things at the Thrift for 50p! I put my outfits together using ideas from fashion blogs and mags and somehow it just works.

4. Sometimes I have panic attacks, but I don't know how to explain them to people (see: worried that people will think I'm mad), so I call them migraines. I do sometimes get migraines too, but not so many headaches as just overall buzzing feelings of doom, which isn't exactly the same thing.

5. I'm really, really scared of dogs. Even though I'm sure yours is lovely, I still shiver when I read his name in your messages.

6. I keep all my fingernails after I clip them off because I read something somewhere how people can take pieces of old nails and things and make voodoo dolls of you and actually wreck your life. I know it isn't true, it can't be! But I still can't throw them out.

7. I don't have any friends my own age at all. The people in my class completely ignore me because I've always been friends with Fi and Chlophie and them, and they're all fourteen. Don't ever tell them, but sometimes I feel like I'm more of a sort of stylish pet for them than a person. Like one of those dogs that celebs carry round in their handbags! When I start feeling that way, I get stroppy with them. I try not to, because it's not their fault they were born two and a bit years sooner than I was! But I can't help it.

8. Since Nan died, I've wondered a bit if it wouldn't be better to be dead too. I think about it, being dead or getting to be dead, but then I stop because if I'm dead,

I'll never meet Nate and you. Nate and you are keeping me alive! Nate and you *and* Fi *and* because I'd feel too guilty about Mum, if I went too. She'd blame herself and I'd feel awful about that. Besides, I don't know enough people yet, so no one would come to my funeral, and it would all be bleak and awful, and Hawkster and Angus would probably graffiti my coffin.

9. This is the worst one. And I'm only telling you because you're my sister. It's that . . . well, sometimes I wish my mum wasn't my mum. She's brilliant at art, but she's a pretty terrible mum. She means well, I know she does, it's just that she hasn't a clue what she's doing. It was Nan who taught me to read and took me to school and went to my school meetings and things. Mum never knew what time anything was on and she didn't seem to mind if she missed it. She'd just laugh about it and say it wasn't important and she didn't understand that it was important to me. Mum just thinks that childhood doesn't much matter because you forget it all, and things that aren't missed aren't things that can possibly matter, because — after all — you'd miss them. It's a bit like your Buddhism, I suppose, except different. More flighty.

And Mum leaves me alone all the time now! She says I'm grown up. But I'm not grown up a bit. I just fake it with clothes and makeup. Sometimes I wish she'd say, 'Look, don't wear that, it's not for children'.

But she doesn't, she doesn't even really notice, I don't think. And sometimes I get really scared here alone and I have to turn the telly to the kids' channel very loud so that it isn't scary anymore. I know the shows are rubbish, but at least they aren't scary. She doesn't seem to twig that without Nan here, I'm just on my own. She doesn't seem to know how much I miss her.

Fi says that Mum is rushing me through my childhood so that I can grow up as fast as she did. Mum had me (us, I suppose) when she was only 21. She got married at 20! That's only six years older than Fi. She says it's because she knew that Dad was the One. It must have been hard, to be a mum AND a widow when she was still really a young person who just wanted to do her art and be famous and things. But why would she want me to be LIKE her? She doesn't seem very happy, not ever. Being a mum and being a proper grown-up all seem a little bit outside of what she was designed to do, which was to do her art and be up all night painting and sometimes to sleep all day and to forget to eat anything except for toast and a million cups of tea.

10. (*This* is worse than that other worst one. If anyone found out about this one, I'd die! I would.) But you asked, so I should explain. It's about the Mole. (Ed.) The thing is that I snogged him after Nan's funeral. This is a *hugely massive secret* of epic proportions! No one

in the world knows. Fi's the only one I could tell. Chloe and Sophie would just fall about laughing and that would be embarrassing. But Fi *hates* her brother. And I do too! Hating the Mole is just what we've always done, ever since I first met Fi. She calls him the Mole because he lurks about in the dark, staring at computer screens. She's being a bit cruel, really, but he *is* her brother. During meals and things, he's always looking off into the distance, as though something very interesting is happening about five metres behind the person talking and they are *really* boring him and he'd rather just get up from the table to go and check out the interesting thing. Which doesn't exist.

I can't think WHY I snogged him, but it must have been because grief does funny things to people. It was right after Nan's funeral, during the cemetery part. I was by myself, waiting while Mum chatted with our neighbour. The Mole came right up to me, in this funny black suit that was too small, showing his ankles and everything. And he said, 'I'm sorry 'bout your nan, Ruby', in this really kind voice that I wasn't expecting to hear from him. I don't know where Fi was. I thought, 'Gosh, what a lovely voice'. I'd never heard him speak before, not even once. Usually when he talks to Fi, he just sort of growls at her and she makes a pretend dog barking noise back. It's their thing that they do.

So, anyway, then I burst into tears. The ugly kind, where

there's snot dripping down and all that. I felt like I couldn't breathe! He grabbed my hand and led me round back, behind the garage where they keep the grave-digging equipment. Then I thought about the grave-digging equipment and I cried even harder. He sat me down on a bench and started rubbing my back. Eventually, I stopped crying, and suddenly, I was just very sleepy, like I had to put my head down and fall asleep right away. So I put my head on his shoulder.

We sat like that for quite a bit. The sounds of the funeral seemed very far away. I could hear talking and, unbelievably, laughing. Like people were at a garden party and not a service for someone who died tragically and horribly and unfairly. I almost started crying again, but he said, 'Don't'.

And then he kissed me. Just like that. It was actually a bit nice, now that I think of it. It was the only time I've ever kissed anyone. Ever.

Apart from the embarrassing note, he hasn't spoken to me since. I should have known he was awful. 'No social skills', Fi would say. 'Or maybe he's a vampire. And that's why he hangs about in the dark all day. Either way, *evil*'.

I don't know if I want to hit Send! I've never sent anything like this to anyone else before. But I will. I'll send it to you. Because you're my twin, and we shouldn't have secrets, should we. We won't. Let's just decide that. To not have any secrets, not between us. OK?

Write me back, Ruth Quayle, and tell me some more of your secrets, and then pretty soon, we'll feel like this is normal. We'll feel like this is how it's always been.

Love,

Ruby

PS — I've attached a picture of the Mole so you can see what he looks like.

FROM: Fiona fififionafifi@aol.co.uk

TO: Ruby Starling starling_girl@mail.com

Rube, these last few days were the best!! Thank you!!!!!! I can *totally* see us being roommates when we go to design school in Paris. It'll be fab. I'll wait for you! It's only a couple of extra years anyway. I'll get a job in a café and learn French and fall in love with a glamorous French *garcon*. Mum says it's amazing we can hang around together so much and never even have a spat, and it is. Before you came along and we got to be such good friends, I was always having tiffs with Chlophie.

I'd trade the Mole in for you in a heartbeat! The vile, dark-dwelling beast. I wonder if we could just swap you out and then you'd be my sister and he could live with your mum. She'd probably not even notice that it happened for at least a fortnight or until the sculpture is finished, whichever comes first. She'd like the Mole. He's low maintenance.

I have to go and pack. I can't believe we're going on a caravan holiday. It's so horrid, there are no words for how horrid. I'll be back in time for Sophie's birthday bash. It'll be amazeog, am sure. Her mum is brill at parties and Chloe's bursting with some revenge plot for Hawkster and Angus.

Oh, Dad's shouting at me from the front door. I'M COMING, DAD! I mean, I'm not, as I haven't packed yet, but don't tell Dad. xo

---

FROM: **Ruth Quayle** iamruthquayle@gmail.com

TO: **Jedgar Allen Johnston** JedgarAllenPoe@yahoo.com

I was flipping around the channels on the TV in the middle of the night last night while eating a bag full of black jelly beans, and getting a little nauseated from either the flipping or the jelly beans, when I landed on *SHARKTOPUS!* Jedgar, someone has stolen our idea! Except of course it isn't a shark/orca hybrid, it's a shark/octopus hybrid! Which, if you think about it, doesn't have any of the chilling intelligence of a shark/orca hybrid, so is not alike at all. I haven't written the voice-over yet, but don't worry, I'm on it. I mean, I'm thinking about it, which is the first step in writing anything, you know. Only the last, tiniest part of writing is spent actually typing something on your laptop.

Jedgar, I don't know what's wrong with me. I feel like I am full of an electric current that won't stop charging, and if I flick my hands, sparks might fly off the ends of my fingertips like fireflies. I am shivering with excitement, or maybe I have the flu, or maybe I just feel all strange and current-y and electrical because I have a twin sister who exists in England and I now actually know who my biological parents are. In fact, using a genealogy website, I have traced my lineage all the way back to A PRINCE IN FRANCE! Can you even believe that? This whole thing is crazy! It turns out that my dad's last name was French, and then my birth mom translated it to Starling, and then I was adopted by someone named Quayle? It's like an entire flock of names, which are now flapping around in my skull, looking for a way out. But there isn't one. There is just me, with a bunch of thoughts that won't stop. I am half French! I have a family tree! I have a history! It's like reading the most interesting book that I've ever read in my entire life, except I am the main character.

Jedgar, do you think I should try to contact my French relatives? Or meet the English ones first? I've talked Mom and Dad into taking our summer trip to England, even though we only have five days and they have pointed out that we will waste two of them traveling, but three days in England meeting my twin sister and my biological mom

seems like ENOUGH TO BLOW MY MIND COM-
PLETELY ANYWAY JEDGAR OMG THIS IS MY LIFE!

OK, good night for now, Jedgar Johnston.

Ruth

FROM: Ruth Quayle iamruthquayle@gmail.com

TO: David Quayle docdaddave@gmail.com ;
Gen Quayle Gen@usdinolab.org

Dear Mom and Dad,

I feel completely terrible that you two are sad, so TOMOR-
ROW NIGHT, do not make any plans for dinner. I am
going to make hamaroni. And I hate hamaroni! So that tells
you how much I love you and also need you to stop acting
weird around me because if you really think about it, what
does it matter that I have a twin in England? Except for it
being one of the coolest things that's happened to anyone
ever at any time, obvi. I am so excited that you've agreed to
go to England for our summer trip. It means more to me
than everything in the whole world all put together. You are
the BEST. Srsly.

Mom, I took your advice, and I'm trying really really
hard to become better friends with Tink Aaron-Martin. I
thought you should know that. It's hard to just go ahead and
make friends with someone. I don't know what else to do

other than skateboard with her when she's at the park and show her stuff. Should I call her? Should I tell her I have a twin sister in England? I've just realized that I don't know how normal people have normal friends, because I've always just had Jedgar and Jedgar is sort of mostly enough.

Anyway, I absolutely need you to give me useful friend-making pointers as well as to be my mom, in just the regular way, that has nothing to do with the fact that Delilah Starling exists. Let's talk about all of this over hamaroni, just like olden times before all of this stuff came tumbling out of the universe and landed square on top of our heads.

Mom, can you leave me the recipe for Hamaroni Surprise?

Love,

Ruth

FROM: **Gen Quayle** Gen@usdinolab.org

TO: **Ruth Quayle** iamruthquayle@gmail.com

Ruth,

I am so sorry if I made you feel like I'm upset with you! I promise I'm not and I can *completely* see how it would be exciting to have a twin. If I'd had a twin when I was a kid,

I would have made her do all the hard things I didn't like and wasn't good at, like gymnastics. I don't know why I think she'd be good at things I was terrible at, it just seems like that would be fair. I think this is all amazing. And that's the truth.

Daddy and I were just talking about what we can do to get information from the agency, who have written back and said that closed adoptions are still closed and can't be reopened for reasons like this one. He wants to hire a lawyer but I think we should just wait it out. At this point, what can they tell us that we don't already know? We can piece together the story by just asking Delilah directly now. I'll leave that up to you, Ruth. This is your other family. It's your roots. It must be amazing for you.

Why don't I make the hamaroni with you? It's not that I don't trust you to cook, it's just that the last time you did, you set a dishcloth on fire and threw it on the curtains and we had to replace the entire wall. Luffetta has enough problems right now without also being lit on fire. I'm coming home early today, so it works out perfectly! I'll bring everything we need to make dinner.

Love you more than a root-beer float on a hot day,

Mommy

MOM, it's MOM. Not MOMMY.

I AM ALMOST THIRTEEN.

And that's *totes* great that you're going to help me, because I'm a terrible cook!

Love,

Ruth

---

nopoppingballoons.tumblr.com

If it works,
then how will Luffy feel?
Not echoing with the memories
of his ancestors.
Instead, suddenly alive,
in a lab
in the suburbs,
pretending to be OK,
but not knowing what OK
really looks like
for his kind.

JEDGAR, I've had a terrific idea! I'm coming over. Be there or be a rectangle! Ha-ha. That's what my dad would say. Funny, right?

FROM: **Jedgar Allen Johnston** JedgarAllenPoe@yahoo.com

TO: **Ruth Quayle** iamruthquayle@gmail.com

OK, but it's crazy here because everyone is packing for our camping trip. We have enough stuff to survive in the wild for two years. Mom is right now holding up a pair of snow pants and saying, "Remember that year when it rained and we were freezing? Should I bring these?" And Dad has managed to pack the entire barbecue. It takes up the whole backseat. I guess we'll have to ride on the roof rack. We have to leave in about two hours, so I hope whatever you want to do isn't something that takes a long time.

I almost had a chance to talk to Mum tonight. She came home for tea and everything, and we were just going to sit down when the phone rang. Mum answered and right away, she got all upset. It was like someone dropped a black cloud directly behind her eyes and all the light was gone. I could tell she was nearly crying, but she didn't want to let on.

It turns out that someone painted something rude on my bottom. Not MINE, but on the sculpture that's finally been moved from her studio to the site at the library for the finishing details. It says MINGER. I don't think Americans use that word, do they? It's a word to describe someone really ugly and awful. Mum is going back with a couple of her artist mates to clean it up, then they're going to build a Perspex 'safety box' around the statue. It sounds like an aquarium, but without the water. I'm trying not to think about the statue-me struggling for air in a box. It'd be a bit like being buried alive, I'd think. Awful.

Ruby

Dear Nan,

I know it's been a few days since I've written to you. How are you? I'm fine.

I'm not really fine. I've been at Fi's, as you know, which was lovely, but now I'm back home, with Mum, except she's had to go back to the library again because someone *vandalised* the statue. Just when she was going to be finished, Nan! I'm pretending that I don't think it was Angus and he did it because of me, but I think it *was* Angus and he *did* do it because of me! Mum said that he came round again while she was working. She said something like 'How are things going with my gorgeous daughter'? And she said he got cross and kicked over her tin of varnish all over the place. Took her ages to clean it up. I don't think she thinks he's so romantic anymore!

I wanted to go with her to help her fix the statue, but she refused, which was horrid, because I also wanted to go so I wouldn't have to be here by myself. What if Angus wants to take revenge on the REAL me? And revenge for what? What a git. Besides, obviously idiots are going to ruin anything nice in this place anyway. Look at the graveyard! And the church! Everything's spray-painted, even your headstone now. I tried to scrub it off, but it didn't work. It's like someone's let monkeys loose with the entire aisle of paints from Homebase.

Love you and miss you more than anything,
Ruby

FROM: **Ruth Quayle** iamruthquayle@gmail.com

TO: **Ruby Starling** starling_girl@mail.com

RUBY, I have some news, which is that Mom and Dad have agreed that we will come to England for our vacation this summer, which is so much better than CAMPING (and even Disneyland!), it's nearly ridic. England! And YOU. You don't have to worry about anything, because we'll stay in a hotel.

The Mole is actually super cute. I have no idea why you call him the Mole! He's completely adorable and if he wanted to snog me in a cemetery, I would probably let him, although maybe not, because I'm not sure I am ready for any sort of snogging yet. Or kissing, as we call it here in America. "Snog" is a funny word.

When I read about the Mole and then your other secrets, I realized that I am completely boring and no wonder I don't have lots of friends who want to borrow my clothes and go to parties. I don't kiss people and I am not in love with any-one, not even a pop star. I like skateboarding. I work really hard at school to keep up. I am trying to make new friends.

I LOVE horror movies. My best friend is a boy named Jedgar. My parents are smart, funny, and basically awesome, even when they are having fridge-arguments. Example: Dad's quote on the board by the fridge today says, "To understand everything is to forgive everything." Mom has written underneath it, "I forgive you for not getting milk but I don't understand why you can't remember it, if it's all I've told you to get." And then Dad has written, "I got distracted by the sale on macaroni!" And Mom has written, "You can't drink macaroni." That actually kind of made my day. I love them. They are crazy weirdos, but they are great.

There just isn't much more. That's all I have. That's who I am.

I sort of feel like I'm letting you down with that, with the lack of snogging, like you're ahead of me. Is that ridic? Please say it is, because I know it is. I just need for you to say it too.

Have you talked to your mum yet? I don't mean to pressure you, but I don't get why you can't just say it. Now that we are almost for SURE coming to England — it's not like we have tickets yet, but when we do, then it will be totes definite — she'll have to know before I show up at the door, beaming happily at you and scaring her to death. And maybe if I understood why she gave me away, I could forgive her and then I'll be not angry and all Buddhist-peaceful-ish and becoming the path that I'm walking on and so on and so forth!

Ruth

Fi,

Remember how, a long time ago, I had the chicken pox and I got really sick, with a high fever and everything? It was so itchy! There was one in my ear that I couldn't scratch and I kept jabbing it with a knitting needle and accidentally punctured my eardrum, which made me so dizzy I couldn't even walk. Mum was a wreck, but luckily Nan was still alive, and she took me to A&E. I had to stay overnight! Anyway, Mum was so worried that she sat by my bed all night and held my hand and confessed things, like how she feels like a complete failure for not getting remarried and giving me a proper dad, not just a picture of one in a frame, with a French family who shun us and our barbarian ways. She cried and hugged me so hard, I thought my ribs would break.

Anyway, Fi, I'm thinking maybe if I said I was feeling poorly, then I could ask her about Ruth without it being so much like an attack. What do you think?

Ruby

No, never mind, that's a terrible plan. Mum's *awful* with ill people. She'd probably do a runner, like when I fell off my bike in the car park where I was learning to cycle and broke my arm. She thought for sure I would haemorrhage and that a blood clot would form and get somehow tossed into my lungs, and the next thing you'd know, I'd be collapsed on the kitchen floor with a trickle of blood coming from my mouth. Nan had to take me to the GP, and Mum went on an art retreat in St Ives for six weeks because even looking at the cast made her upset! I can't have her go off again.

Are you reading this? Do they have the Internet in Wales? I only ask because you've stopped sending me pics. Do pirates attack caravans? Have you been kidnapped by evildoers? Please reply!

RUUUUUBY, where have you been? We came round earlier and knocked and knocked and no one answered. It's TERRRR-RRRIBLE about the statue. Your poor mum! We saw her earlier and she's put you into a plastic box and someone's already written on the outside of the box with a Sharpie! Won't tell you what it says, 'cause it's not about you, it's just because whoever wrote it probably had a crap childhood and is angry with the whole world. Saw that on a chat show last night, that graffiti painters are all from broken homes and tragic pasts. Your past is a bit tragic too, specially now that you have an American twin! Maybe you're secretly the spray-painter!

'Course, we KNOW it's not you. Anyway, come round when you can, we're at Soph's doing henna tattoos all over our arms and legs. Trouble is, the ones on our legs look like hair! But it doesn't come off, so we're going to spray-tan until you can't see it anymore. Don't you just love getting all brown and gorgeousy-gorgeous? It's so summery. Come if you like! xo

I think I know what you mean about snogging the Mole making me ahead of you, but it's not like that, because I also know what you mean about not feeling ready, and I know that I'm not. Not to snog the Mole or to snog ANYONE. I don't even want to.

Do you really think he's nice-looking? Maybe he is and I just never noticed because Fi's always going on about how terrible he smells and how he drinks the milk straight out of the carton and puts it back in the fridge, all spitty and so on. I do think that maybe if I'd done that self-defence class with him then he'd have talked to me more, and maybe we could have got to know each other a little bit. As friends, like you and Jedgar are friends. Then I remembered that he's never said another word to me except, 'Sorry about your nan', and likely we'd just be kicking at the dummies and punching them in silence and afterwards he'd roll his eyes at me and walk away. Probably for the best, then.

Are you actually coming? That's so exciting. (Exciting in the way that you're excited when you're in the queue to go on the London Eye and then it's your turn and you suddenly realise how high up it goes and how you can't get off until the ride is over, even if you want to. Scary. But exciting mostly.) Can you tell me exactly when? I need to know. It's not like we're planning to go anywhere, but Mum might suddenly decide she needs to go on a course on grieving or brushstrokes or glass blowing or home organisation and leave town. It would be terrible if the timing was wrong and she wasn't even here.

Do you ever listen to STOP? If you don't, you really should, because their words are basically just like poetry and I know you're a poet and love poems and all that. Anyway, in the new single, Nate sings, 'No one really knows me, even when I show them who I am'. Isn't that brill? That's how I feel about everything right now. And everyone. Everyone but you, maybe. Because for the first time ever, I feel like someone actually *does* understand me.

Love,
Ruby

FROM: **Ruby Starling** starling_girl@mail.com

TO: **Delilah Starling** theartistdelilah@yahoo.co.uk

Mum, everyone says that the Perspex box looks fantastic, so well done. I know it's not real, but I still wish there were airholes so that the statue-me can breathe. I know that's silly. Are you going to be home for tea today? I'll make some bacon sandwiches. It's just that we REALLY need to talk, Mum, truly.

Love,
Ruby

FROM: **Delilah Starling** theartistdelilah@yahoo.co.uk

TO: **Ruby Starling** starling_girl@mail.com

Darling, that's lovely. I love bacon sandwiches. They're the perfect food. Nan loved them too, didn't she? Some days I miss her so much, especially when I'm done with a project and it's getting so much attention. I won't be home for tea, that's the thing, because someone from the *Guardian* is coming up to do a bit about the statue and the library extension and they want me on camera. We'll have to make sure to buy a paper on the weekend and not forget. I'll just have something to eat here, but wait up for me, darling.

Lots of love,
Delilah (Mummy)

Mum says I can't take any more calls on the mobile, but we've stopped at an Internet café, so I can write to you, FINALLY. Chloe's making me mad with all these e's she's sending about Sophie's party. I think she's got your email addy wrong though, so you probably haven't even been getting them! Can you call Chloe and tell her I've dropped the phone in the sea and that the Welsh don't use computers like the rest of the entire world? I haven't chucked the phone, but Mum's going to do it for me if it doesn't stop beeping with messages all night long. Plus it hasn't got any more memory for pictures and I don't know how to make space and the Mole won't help me because he's a complete wazzock, as you know. Sophie's mum will do something brilliant for that party anyway, so I don't know why Chloe has her knickers in a twist. Soph's mum is a party *planner*! It'll be fab! Chloe doesn't have to do ANYTHING but show up! It'll be the first, real, proper, excellent party we've ever had as mid-teens. Chlophie have decided that 15 is officially mid, so there should be a word, like preteen, teen, mid-teen, and then young adult. Gosh, seems funny that we'll all be mid-teens and you'll only barely be a teen!

Speaking of Chlophie, did they tell you that the date they went on with Hawkster and Angus was actually a BET? All the boys were in on it. They had a whole betting sheet on whether or not the boys could snog the girls. Chlophie are awfully upset but pretending not to be, like they do. Chloe says that Soph never thought Hawkster was even a tiny bit cute and she, Chloe, knew all along that Angus was a prat, because of what he wrote to you, but she was only going along to support Soph. But Soph says that Chloe was getting keen on Angus, after all, but she just didn't want to tell you because of how stroppy you get and how you thought he was an horrid email writer who lurched around your mum's art being creepy with spray paint. Anyway, they're awfully miffed and surely about to do something mental to get revenge. You should find out what! I can't do anything from Wales. It's like being on another planet.

Anyway, BIG NEWS. We're coming back early because Dad's cousin's wife's son is moving to England with his family, only they aren't coming over till September so he's going to stay with us for the first bit of school. He's AMER-ICAN, and he's close to your age. I think he's only 13! He's got the worst name ever: Berk. How could anyone call a baby 'Berk'? They may as well call him 'Minger'. But you'll like him! He looks a bit like Nate, Ruby, when you look at him straight on. So it's like he's your destiny. I *can't* fancy him because he's related AND younger than me, even though he's not actually a *blood* relly.

Did you hear from Ruth again? Your plan about being ill is terrible but you already knew that, so I needn't say anything, actually. You probably should just ask her, straight up.

Miss you!

FROM: **Ruth Quayle**   iamruthquayle@gmail.com

TO: **Jedgar Allen Johnston**   JedgarAllenPoe@yahoo.com

I'm sorry. Or MEA CULPA. Or whatever is the right thing to say.

I was hanging out with Tink Aaron-Martin instead of you because 1) she's funny and nice and why shouldn't I? And 2) because now that I have a twin sister, I feel like it's my duty to have more friends who are girls so I can understand how other girls are and how they think. And 3) because Mom wants me to have girl friends instead of just you and I feel like with all this stuff about my biological mom, it's the least I can do for her. It's not like I talk to Tink about Ashley Mary Jane's heart, or my mysterious English twin, or being adopted or anything. We just skateboard around and give each other high fives and she pretends that she's not looking at that blue-haired kid over my shoulder. I think she has a crush on him, and she'll probably tell me about it pretty soon because we're sort of almost real, actual friends.

And anyway, whatever, Jedgar. Why are YOU mad? It's not like you weren't chatting up Freddie Blue Anderson over by the slides because she's pretty and has good hair, and in spite of the fact she has the personality of a piece of rotting cheese. You've been weird ever since you got back from camping. Did something happen that you're not telling me? I think something must have. What's going on?

FROM: **Chlophie!!!** chlophie@hotmail.co.uk

TO: **Ruby Starling** starling_girl@mail.com

Cor, I can't BELIEVE you've missed the things I forwarded to you about Soph's do! Why didn't you say they weren't coming through!? I changed the *R* in your name to a *T*, quite by accident, and didn't notice. I just got this really angry note from someone named Bonnie Statling Anderson who says that if we don't stop right away, she's going to report us to INTERPOL. Which would be exciting, wouldn't it? Wonder if they can throw people in some kind of international gaol for sending party messages to a wrong email addy? That'd be amazeog! Imagine! A gaol full of people who can't type, wandering about crying, 'But I meant it to be an *R*'!

Anyway, instead of sending them on, I'll summarise, yeah? Because you've got other stuff to worry about, like your twin in America and the fact that someone has taken away your Perspex and now you're all out there in the library square, waiting to be painted on by some wazzock.

Anyway, I've got Skinny Kate in on the revenge plan, because Angus, that spotty git, doesn't know we're mates. (D'you know her? She's in our year at school but she's very quiet and funny, in a nerdy sort of way.) She's been interviewing him regularly at the chip shop. She told him she was practising to be a journo when she grows up, so we've all the facts, such as: He has a Siamese fighting fish named Horace, and he is deeply afraid of changing lightbulbs. Somehow we'll work that into the revenge plan that Sophie can only know part of, right? Gosh, this is difficult. How can I do this without telling her about the party? Please don't tell her. Make sure you don't copy her on this by accident, then it will just be ruined, won't it?

Love you! Kisses, dahling.

Chloe and Sophie

PS — Actually, it's just from me, Chloe, but Soph insisted I sign her name too, because she didn't want to write to you herself AND she doesn't know what I'm typing over here in the corner. Oohhhhh, I mean, 'her nail varnish is still wet'. YES, I ALREADY TOLD HER ABOUT ANGUS AND HAWKSTER, SOPH. RELAX. DON'T READ OVER MY SHOULDER, IT'S RUDE. Bye Ru-Ru!

But you didn't forward me any of the things, so I still don't know about the Thing You Asked Me Not To Say Anything About, and Chloe, how do you know that Soph won't read the emails if you share an addy?

Fi told me about Hawkster and Angus and the bet. I think you should just forget about it and never speak to them again. They aren't worth the trouble, they really aren't. Wazzocks. (Wazzock is my new fav word, actually. Suits all of them.)

Fi, I'm so glad you're coming back early! Hurrah! I've missed you more than anything. But I'm absolutely *not* going to fancy your cousin. I don't have time for boys. I *really* have to deal with Mum. She came home tonight and was lying about being dramatic about the vandalism, talking about the 'scourge of British society' and their 'disrespect for fine arts', and trying to sign us up for that self-defence class your dad was on about last month! I told her it was already over, but she doesn't always pay any mind to what I say. Besides, is she planning to stand beside the statue and ward people off with her fists?

I tried, I really *did* try to talk to her about Ruth, Fi, but everything I said came out all wrong and jumbled up, and then she got in the bath. I followed her into the bathroom and then she looked at me with such a proper look of caring that I burst into tears and had to run out because I couldn't talk without crying. Then I chickened out. It's just that she's so upset about a STATUE. How is she going to be when I mention that there is an actual LIVE other version of me? Not just an art version that keeps getting scribbled on with Sharpies? What if she can't cope? Then what?

Ruth's going to be here SOON. I don't know exactly when, because she hasn't said yet, but . . . soon is soon.

FROM: Ed kingsupereddie@gmail.com

TO: Ruby Starling starling_girl@mail.com

We're on our holiday. It's OK, I guess. Ghosts and paranormal things are big here. Dad's really into it. Says the ghosts have all the answers. They know who did it. Guess Dad supposes everyone was murdered. Do you believe in ghosts and things? Don't know if I do, but it's hard not to here. Crucifixes in everyone's window and the like and lots of businesses doing tours. We haven't seen a ghost. You probably think it's funny, me writing like this to you. It is. I've never written to a girl before. Never wanted to. You're the first one. Wish you'd write back, Ruby. At least tell me to go away. Maybe when I'm back, we could talk or something. Don't know how you'd tell Fi, though. Well, she wants the iPad back now. I'll have to send quick and delete. Tonight we're going on a cemetery tour. Makes me think of you. Sounds creepy, right? I don't mean it like that. This is stupid. Just write back if you like.

Ed

FROM: **Fiona** fififionafifi@aol.co.uk

TO: **Ruby Starling** starling_girl@mail.com

I've got the iPad away from the Mole! He's been typing something mysterious all morning. And when I grabbed it, he snatched it back before I could see. Could the Mole be writing to a GIRL??? Mystery! Anyway, I told Dad I was reading *Sherlock Holmes* on the ebook app and he thinks that's a jolly good use of time, so I just have to lie on the lounger a bit crookedly so he can't tell that I'm really typing.

Look, I've come up with a brill plan. Why don't you just not say anything? Just stick a pic of Ruth somewhere, one that obviously *isn't* you, and then see what she does or if she even reacts at all. I know from reading proper whodunits that perps always have tells — reactions that give them away. She'll have to say something, then. She can't run away from a picture. She can't avoid knowing that you know. And she can't do that thing she sometimes does where she pretends it doesn't matter or she'll deal with it later. I don't know HOW she does that, actually, it's like she skims over important things so quickly you don't even know it's happening. But this will stop her in her tracks. She'll see it and then it WILL matter. And she won't be able to pretend it doesn't.

See you SOON!

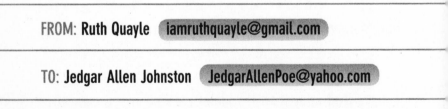

FROM: **Ruth Quayle**   iamruthquayle@gmail.com

TO: **Jedgar Allen Johnston**   JedgarAllenPoe@yahoo.com

I know it's 3 a.m., but I've just realized that we have to ask Ruby if it's OK to make this documentary, because it's about her too. If she finds out that I've told you some of her secret things to use in the animated part, she'll be so angry, she'll never speak to me again, and I'll deserve it because I said I wouldn't tell and I did! Maybe you could not use those parts. Please don't use those parts. JEDGAR, IF YOU USE THOSE PARTS, YOU WILL RUIN MY LIFE.

Jedgar, *call* me as soon as you wake up. The trouble with documentaries is that they are true and about real people and real feelings, and so I think all the real people involved should know.

Ruth

FROM: **Ruby Starling** starling_girl@mail.com

TO: **Fiona** fififionafifi@aol.co.uk

Fi, I don't know. But I don't have any better ideas, so I suppose I can try. What's the worst that can happen? It seems so jarring, though! But you're right about how she skims. It's like trying to talk to a cloud. Whenever I think, 'Oh, I'll say something now' she just wafts away.

I can't wait for you to be home. When you're away, I've no one to properly talk to. I've missed you! See you soon-ish?

You stop talking about your twin
because you saw Mom's chin tremble
when she ripped open the cheese packet
and it spilled orange dust on the floor.

Among the cheese dust on the floor
lie all your feelings about how your
real actual mom
gave you away
because you were broken
and because your real actual dad
died in a car crash.

"My whole life has been
decided by car accidents,"
you say.
And she doesn't answer
because maybe she didn't hear you
or maybe you didn't say it
out loud
after all.

Ruth,

I'm at work but I just remembered that Tink called earlier to talk to you. You should call her back. She sounds funny and kind, just like YOU.

Dad is booking the tickets for England for the twenty-first. It's the only date that works for his job and mine, so we'll have to figure out how to cram all the meetings-with-your-family into only a couple of days. We'll go again, I promise. And maybe a couple of days are enough for now.

How's *SHORCA!*? Can't WAIT to see it. You're so smart. I knew my daughter would be amazing. And look at you:

You are.

Love you more than a surprise vacation in the Hawaiian Islands during a cold snap at home,

Mom

P.S. Please shut off the computer and go to bed now. I know I am terrible at reinforcing bedtime, but I just read this study about how kids who don't get enough sleep can get anxious, and we'd hate for that to happen to you.

I'm *already* anxious, Mom.

Good night!

Love,

Ruth

Sometimes when I think about you and I being *twins*, and all that *that* means, from being scrunched together inside Mum and splitting cells and being really the same person, my heart starts beating strangely, maybe like yours. It feels like a bird that's stuck on flypaper, all trapped and doomed, flapping his wings around to try to escape.

I saw a bird stuck like that once. It was at this party that we had in the back garden, where Mum was marrying herself last year after she decided that boyfriends were never going to measure up to Dad. I know that sounds barking, but it was really lovely. She looked amazing! And so happy.

But then things got weird when one of her ex-boyfriends showed up and started shouting, 'Oi! Well, ain't this a pretty picture? She wouldn't marry me, would she? But marry 'erself, she will'? Fi's dad took care of him, but the mood was ruined. Mum went inside to regroup in the bath, so Fi and I cleaned up, and that's when we found the bird. I think I killed him by mistake when I tried to pull him free.

The poems on your tumblr make me feel like I did when that bird died. D'you know what I mean?

I just wanted to tell you that. I think some things are going to happen soon. I've done something. I've done something that will make Mum tell me everything, I think.

Love,
Ruby

FROM: **Ruby Starling**   starling_girl@mail.com

TO: **Fiona**   fififionafifi@aol.co.uk

I know you probably won't get this e, Fi, but I did what you said and Sellotaped a picture of Ruth with all her tubes and hospital things to the fridge. I hope it's not a terrible mistake. I'm so nervous, I can hear my heart beating. It's beating like it's taking up the whole room, like those tribal drums they made us listen to in World Cultures, d'you remember?

The ones that felt like they were beating all the way through us, from our feet all the way to our hair.

FROM: **Ruth Quayle** iamruthquayle@gmail.com

TO: **Ruby Starling** starling_girl@mail.com

Ruby,

What you said about the bird and the flypaper was *totes* absolutely amazingly flabbergastingly poetic. You have a poetic soul, like me. Mom and Dad don't really *get* poetry, so I don't tell them that I write it. (Also, it's private!) (And often about them!) And if they read it, they'd probably laugh by mistake or just — worse! perish the thought! — not understand it.

ALSO, I HAVE DATES: We are coming to England on August 21. At least, we leave on the 21st, but weirdly we arrive on the 22nd at 11:35 in the morning, not that I expect you to come to London to meet us or anything. I just thought you should know!

Write back AS SOON AS SOMETHING HAPPENS, if it happens, and also, tell me what you DID. I'm going to write another poem now. Suddenly, I feel all poemy. Like they are scrabbling around inside me, hoping to come out.

the air is humming
with something that's like music
but fainter
music that is getting
louder in your veins
the trumpets that say
something is about
to happen
that you can't take
back.

FROM: **Ruth Quayle**   iamruthquayle@gmail.com

TO: **Jedgar Allen Johnston**   JedgarAllenPoe@yahoo.com

Dear Jedgar,

I realize you are probably abandoning our documentary about my life because you have fallen in love with Freddie Blue Anderson and are too busy to trouble yourself with my story, mine and Ruby's. Well, fine. I'm so super mad at you for not telling me that when you went camping, she was there too, and now you love her and she loves you, except I don't know if she does. She's mean, in case you didn't notice.

And I am very hurt, Jedgar. Not because I wanted you to *love* me — I'm not ready for anything like that AND I have a lot going on right now anyway — but because of the movie, which was important to me. It was taking this whole weird chapter of my life and turning it into something that I could actually manage to hold on to, instead of having it flap up and away, out of my reach. It was going to do that for me. Somehow. I don't even know how! That's just how I felt! And now I feel betrayed by your PERFIDIOUS act!

Jedgar Johnston, I am having a panic attack! Like, a real one! I am breathing very fast! And my heart is pounding! And it's your fault! Tink told me. She told me that FBA and you were camping together. She told me everything. And anyway, I saw the way you were making googly eyes at her at the skate park and then I pretended it wasn't a big deal and we're just friends, which we are, but it's still a big deal.

OK.

OK.

I am trying to calm down. But Jedgar, you can't just do that, go frolicking off to the beach with Freddie Blue Anderson and then avert your eyes when I come up to you. What is happening to you?

This is all sort of my way of saying PLEASE DON'T ABANDON ME, JEDGAR. If that's what you're going to do.

Ruby,

I have insomnia sometimes, which means I can't sleep and I toss and turn and then the blankets and sheets get so looped around me that I have to struggle free, and I wake up from funny little half sleeps breathing really fast. It's scary. So sometimes I just write stuff down, random things, so that I don't have to worry about why I'm breathing so fast and whether Ashley Mary Jane's heart is doing what it needs to do.

I woke up this time having a horrible nightmare about Freddie Blue Anderson. "Who?" you are saying. "Who is that?" Well, I will tell you. FBA is the almost-thirteen-year-old-girl equivalent of fake Christmas trees. Which means she is very pretty from a distance, but up close you realize she is of terrible quality and gratingly fakety fake fake. Her BFF is my new friend, Tink, who is funny, kind, and sweet, and it's a complete mystery why they are friends at all. I heard FBA say once that they met in a past life, where she was an Egyptian princess and Tink was a slave who was called up to duty as the princess's servant. Yes, she really said that! She is the worst of all the worst things you can imagine, and I'm including headless snakes that writhe around on the path in front of you while you are hiking, scaring you into running back to the car at a full sprint and refusing to get out and participate in "hiking" ever again.

Jedgar is very vulnerable to pretty, normal girls because he has always believed he's hideous, because he has one leg shorter than the other, and for his whole life, his brothers have been calling him Limpy. And so he is exactly the kind of boy who would want the validation of a pretty girl liking him, and even possibly not notice that she is a mean and horrible person! *ZUT ALORS!* I have attached a picture that I took of Jedgar this afternoon. You can just see FBA over his shoulder with her sweep of blond hair, looking perfect and horrible.

I do not know why I'm telling you this. I don't want Jedgar to be my boyfriend and I don't want to kiss him and I just really want him to be normal and like he always is, just for the rest of the summer, because everything else is so topsy-turvy. Do you know what I mean?

There's also this other thing I've been meaning to tell you. Well, ASK you, really, and I haven't and I've put it off and now you'll probably be mad. It is: Would it be OK if Jedgar made a small documentary about what it's like to find your twin on the Internet and then accidentally find the mother who abandoned you at birth? Please say yes and please don't be mad that I didn't ask before he started. It's just that I didn't quite know that he was really going to do it, and then suddenly he was working on it, and it all blurred together with *SHORCA!* (our animated short movie about a shark/orca hybrid who is not a psychotic killing machine, but rather a misunderstood and lonely being).

I don't know what it will look like or if he'll even get it all done, but he's collecting facts and one day maybe he'll be able to figure out how to package them all up beautifully into a nice, shiny movie that has a beginning and middle and end. But I can't think how, because mostly this seems like a beginning, and I can't even guess how it will ever be an end.

Love,
Ruth

FROM: **Ruby Starling**   starling_girl@mail.com

TO: **Ruth Quayle**   iamruthquayle@gmail.com

Ruth,

I think Jedgar looks the tiniest bit like Daniel Radcliffe when he was thirteen — not now, when he's obviously an adult man and not suitable crush material for someone who actually IS thirteen. I can see why you could fancy him. I think he only might possibly fall into the trap of liking this FBA creature because she sounds like one of those girls who are all shiny and out there, being popular and having look-at-me hair and always jumping around and ending sentences with question marks and a toss of the head. If he does like her. And you haven't really got any evidence that he does! Do you?

And even if he does, it won't last. We are (almost) thirteen. Nothing lasts when you are thirteen. Actually, I'm coming to think that nothing lasts at all. People die and leave you, or they just leave you anyway. Ask Mum. She'll tell you. And anyway, when FBA ditches him, he'll be back to being your normal friend. You might just have to wait it out.

I'm getting pretty good at waiting things out.

Like right now, I'm waiting for Mum to go into the kitchen.

See, the thing that I did to get Mum to talk was to stick that pic that you sent of you as a baby onto the fridge. Only when she came home last night, after we celebrated the unveiling of the statue, she went straight to bed and didn't go in the kitchen, and then this morning, she left again without seeing it. She's taking the train into London to meet with the bank, which she does every time she finishes a project and gets paid. She doesn't know that she's holding our fate bunched up in her hands, and instead is just breezily carrying on with things like everything is normal!

I feel as if I've let you down. It's not many more days now until you come here and I still haven't told her anything. I still haven't done my bit.

I don't know what to think, really, about Jedgar making a movie. Do you think he'll actually do it? I don't know if I'd want that. What if other people see it? Sometimes I don't want to be seen, not that much.

I'm not angry, though. It's not like that.

Ruby

Ruby to Nan

Dear Nan,

I have made the most terrible, awful, horrid mistake. I can't write it here because I'll just have to write it all over again to Ruth. And I don't much want you to know, actually. I do, but I don't.

I just saw a prism on the glass where the sun was coming in at an angle and it was like there was a rainbow puddle of light pooling on the floor by the door. That was probably you, wasn't it? Saying, 'What on earth were you thinking, you ridiculous girl'?

I'm sorry.

Love,

Ruby

I'm writing this to both of you, even though you don't know each other, just because you'll both want to know and I don't want to type it all twice. I have a migraine that's so huge it's like there is an entire elephant sitting on my head, squeezing my brain into a squidge of jelly.

Mum came home and saw the picture.

When I heard her heels clip-clopping into the kitchen, my heart started beating so fast I thought it would burst right there in my chest, like that little bird's did when I tried to peel him off the flypaper.

Then she screamed like she'd just seen an axe murderer. I ran into the room, and by the time I got there, she was crumpled in a heap on the floor, heaving with sobs and clutching the printout so hard that it was ruined.

'Where did you get this, Ruby'? she kept gasping, between sobs. Then she was sick in the sink.

I said, 'What happened? What is it'? Which made it seem like I didn't *know* what it was and hadn't put it there myself in the first place. Which is awful, really the worst thing. But I couldn't own up! It was too much!

Then after wailing on the floor for quite some time, Mum got up and said, 'Right, then'. And she briskly rang

999 and asked for the POLICE. She said she was reporting a Breaking and Entering. 'Nothing is stolen', she said. 'I don't think. Though I haven't actually looked'. I could tell by the way she said it that the person on the other end of the phone was confused. So was I!

As it happens, your dad was on duty, Fi. We live in a pretty small village, Ruth, so basically he's always on duty, and if it's something particularly troubling, he calls in the real police from the city. He came racing over on his scooter and asked a lot of questions. I couldn't hear them because Mum barricaded the door and shouted at me to go away, so I took a drinking glass and held it up against the wall — which magnifies the sound, as you know — and I still couldn't hear anything, but what I did hear was:

Twins

Adopted

Dead

'What else could I do'? (This part I heard because she shouted it about a dozen times. Or more!)

And then I heard your dad, Fi, and he just said, 'There, there', over and over again. I could tell he felt helpless, but mostly because that's how he usually is when people cry. He gets overwhelmed, right? Maybe all men are like that, hopeless when women sob. Anyway, he must have made a call because next thing I knew, the ambulance was there and Mum was being given something to calm her down. It took ages for them all to go away. Fi, your dad kept wanting me to go home with him. But I knew I had to stay with Mum. She couldn't be alone! And I knew I had to tell her that it was me, after all. It wasn't a break-in.

Finally, they left. Mum slumped over in the old chair that used to belong to Nan. It smells dreadful, like fish and cigarettes, which is specially odd because Nan didn't smoke and she was allergic to seafood. Mum hates that chair, but we kept it because I cried when she said she was going to chuck it now that Nan was gone.

'Mum', I said, 'I'm sorry. It was me. I did it. I put that picture on the fridge'.

She turned as white as a ghost. She kept trying to talk and couldn't.

Finally, she said, 'Oh, Ruby'.

I felt a bit braver then, and I said, 'This has gone on long enough. You obviously had twin daughters and gave one away because she had a manky heart. And you assumed she died? Well, she didn't. Her name is Ruth and she lives in America. She found me on the Internet and we've been talking online for yonks. So tell me everything that happened'.

'She found you on the Internet'? she said, faintly, like her voice was coming from very far away. 'People do that'?

Then she said, 'She's alive? Really'? And she sort of smiled, then she started crying again, really hard. A snotty, awful kind of crying. I didn't know what to do, so I went and sat on the arm of her chair and patted her head, like she was the child and I was the mum. And I said things like, 'It's

OK' and 'I'm sorry', even though I haven't anything to be sorry for and it isn't really OK.

My heart was racing so fast, I thought it might just fly out of my chest and out the open window into the night. My legs were shaking. I felt awful. For her. For me. For all of us.

Then she just said, 'I . . . I . . . I . . . didn't even know you had the Internet. Well, I suppose I did. I must pay for it, right'? She waved her hand vaguely towards the desk where all the bills are stacked up. 'I didn't know the Internet did that, anyway'. Then she said again, 'She's alive'? Then, 'She can't be'. And 'She isn't'.

Then she just said, 'I'm so sorry, darling. I didn't know. I . . . I . . . I . . .'

She said 'I' a whole bunch of times over and over again, and then just like your dad did when you told him, Ruth, she touched her face, like she was checking to make sure it was still there.

Then she started over. 'I can't believe this', she said. 'I feel like I'm having a really strange dream. But it isn't one'! She stood up and then she sank back into the chair. She was smiling in a really peculiar way and murmuring your name, 'Ruth, Ruth, Ruth'. She said it like she was tasting something new and incredible. *Ruth, Ruth, Ruth*.

Then she tried again. 'It's just that Nan told me that she'd died. She said she'd died. She swore that she'd died'.

Then she got out of the chair and held her hands up to the ceiling and she shouted, 'YOU SAID SHE'D DIED'!

Then she started to cry again, an inside-out kind of cry. I was crying too. I didn't know what to do! It was scary and awful and so sad. I felt like all my insides were being torn out of me like pages of a book, then crumpled up and lit on fire. Mum was walking round but she got dizzy. She kept tilting into the walls, kind of blindly, crying and saying, 'Ruth'. It went on for a long time. Ages and ages. It felt like forever, like we were there for days with her crying 'RUTH' and me saying, helplessly, 'It's OK, Mum. Breathe, Mum. It's OK'.

Finally, she sat down, but she kept saying, 'What's happening to me now? What is this? You know, Nan wouldn't let me hold her. Nan said, "Don't do that" when I reached for her. Nan . . .' I wanted her to stop saying that, about Nan, so I said 'SHHHHHH'. And she looked surprised, and she stopped talking. Her eyes were closing. I remembered that when the ambulance was here, they gave her a pill that made her sleepy.

It was really like she was a baby, then. I had to hold her hands and pull her to her bed, and then tucked her up. I kissed her on the forehead, like a mum would. And I told her that it was OK, that she could tell me tomorrow, but she was already asleep.

What happens now?

FROM: Fiona fififionafifi@aol.co.uk

TO: Ruby Starling starling_girl@mail.com

Oh Ruby. Gosh. I don't even know what to say. Want me to come round?

FROM: Ruby Starling starling_girl@mail.com

TO: Fiona fififionafifi@aol.co.uk

I wish I hadn't done it, Fi.

It was your idea.

Maybe I should have just written her an email, so she'd have had time to think about it all properly. I feel like I've hit her on the head with a brick. I'm an awful person! I wanted her to talk with me about it so badly, but I don't think I thought about how shocking it would be for her. I feel so terrible, Fi. What do I do now? And what if she doesn't go back to normal?

I know you're not *really* cross with me, you're just stressed about your mum, but when you said that about how it was my idea, it felt like you were blaming me. It wasn't my doing, it was just an idea! I'm sorry. I'm so sorry, Ruby. You know I wouldn't purposefully do anything to betray you or put you in an awful position or anything like that! You're my best mate!

You know it passes, when she gets like this. Remember? Didn't she do this last year when that horrible man she was dating asked her if she would go to France with him and then left without her, taking your nan's old leather luggage with him? I mean, it wasn't anything the same, but she did cry a whole lot and you had to tell her it was OK. She let you do that, let you take care of her. She's just doing the same thing now. She'll be OK.

But Fi, it's not the same as that at all. It's like she was so used to being upset about men who leave, she almost became like an actress in a film playing the part of someone heartbroken. This time, it was like a tidal wave of *real* feelings. Anyone would have been knocked over by that, not just Mum.

I just hope when she wakes up, she'll be OK. She has to be OK, right?

FROM: Ruth Quayle iamruthquayle@gmail.com

TO: Ruby Starling starling_girl@mail.com

Ruby,

Everything is going to be totes OK. I don't know why I had to say that first, but I did. I do. Because I believe it.

She didn't say it wasn't true. She *did* give me away because of my heart. She let me go because she thought I wouldn't live.

I'm trying really hard, Ruby. I'm trying REALLY hard to think, OK, I can forgive her for that because she was young and her husband had died and she was scared and in America and away from her home in England and everything else that happened, but I don't know if I CAN forgive her for not even holding me, no matter what your nan said. I was a baby! A sick baby! What kind of awful person was your nan, anyway? I thought you said she was lovely! A real, proper mom would have held me until I died. I don't expect you to understand because you didn't die. I'm the one who died. Even though I didn't.

I'm so super scared I can't forgive her, Ruby. I don't think I can! I know I should! I have to! If I don't, I know that I'll be the one who gets all twisted up inside. I know it, not just from Buddha, but because I think I've already gotten twisted up inside just from my whole life, from feeling like I'm not good enough. From, I guess, already being mad at her. I have to let it all go. I just know that I do.

The thing that I know mostly is that we can't change what's already happened. That's what Buddha would say, and anyone really. It's done. When I think about Ashley Mary Jane or the fact I was adopted, I think, "Well, it is what it is" and I feel like basically — you know what I said before about not being a path, but being a river? It means we are all the leaves being pushed along by rivers and we feel like we can't control what happens to us. But we are also the river! All the stuff we think and feel and hate and love and stuff is what decides if the river is terrifying whitewater rapids or just a gentle stream that is perfect for wading where we can bob along in the sunshine, all happy and pretty and safe! It totes makes sense to me now, even though I can't explain it so it doesn't sound like the ramblings of someone crazy: The leaf. The river. Us. All of this. It just IS. All we can do is stay in this very exact minute and not try to guess if there is going to be a waterfall up ahead because we're a leaf. It won't matter anyway. We'll just be carried along to the next calm patch sooner or later, or maybe we'll disintegrate or get eaten by a fish. I'm not sure how that part figures in, come to think of it. I think maybe just to realize that there's no use in anticipating it until it actually happens. So here I am. I am right here, right now breathing. The sun is shining in the window right now and Caleb is lying in the sunbeam and his fur is warm against my feet. And the way the sun is blasting on the screen is making it hard for me to read, and so I'm all squinty.

A squinty river.

A squinty river with hot feet who can smell a stinky dog (did you know that dogs sweat?).

A squinty, hot-footed, bad-scent-sniffing river who is still really mad and sad. Ruby, your mom is a terrible person. I feel bad that she's all you had. Because at least I got a great mom out of the deal, one who would never have said, "Oh, that one will probably die," and walked away. And now she's making YOU be the mom, basically. She's letting you figure it out. And that's just mean. There's something wrong with her, Ruby. It isn't actually OK at all.

The stuff I said about the river only made sense when I was typing it. Buddhism is pretty perplexing, as it turns out. Just when you think you get it, then suddenly, you don't again. I guess not getting it is probably the point, actually. Or at least, part of the point. I just don't know which part.

Ruth

---

nopoppingballoons.tumblr.com

If you have a mom,
you know how her face looks
when she's mad
or sad
or happy.
You know how her breath smells after coffee
or tuna sandwiches.
You know that when she's tired
her left eye squints
and you wonder
what your other mother looks like
when she's mad or sad or happy
or how she smells after
a stinky meal.

This other *mother*
being the woman who
put you down, and said,
"I can't."
Your real mother is the one
who held her arms open
and picked you up.

None of this explains why
though there were two of you,
only one was
saved.

Which one?

FROM: Ruth Quayle `iamruthquayle@gmail.com`

TO: Jedgar Allen Johnston `JedgarAllenPoe@yahoo.com`

I know you haven't answered my last note, but *something has happened.* So can we let bygones be bygones PLEASE and get back to telling each other everything? I need that. So totes pretend I didn't say anything about FBA! She doesn't matter! Not compared to this, which is huge, like a river of

STUFF and FEELINGS that is crushing the leaf version of me flat under its huge, tremendous weight.

It's just that I've found out something, which I sort of already knew, but now I know for sure: My biological mom left me in America because she thought I was going to die.

Jedgar, I can't stop thinking about puppies. When Caleb was born, we got to visit on the first day, and his eyes were still all squinched shut. He couldn't even open them yet. Frankly, he looked like a guinea pig, and I was mostly disappointed because I was little and I thought puppies were born cute, and not actually so pink and rodentlike.

He was the runt. He was basically half the size of all the other puppies and they stomped all over him to get to the mom's milk, and even the mom didn't seem to like him. She kept nosing the runt away from the other dogs. And the breeder said, "Oh, that one will die." And she was so casual about it, like of COURSE the mom-dog would reject the runt-puppy because it didn't matter! It wouldn't survive anyway!

It's exactly the same thing! Do you see that? Delilah Starling nosed me out of the way, grabbed Ruby, and got on a plane and vanished forever.

I am the runt. Just like Caleb.

I want you to put that in the documentary. I just want DELILAH STARLING to hear this part, about the runt-puppy. I want her to feel terrible about it. I want it to break her heart.

Woof,
says the runt.
And her mother
pushes her away,
her huge claws
tearing at the runt's
unopened eyes.

FROM: **Ruby Starling** starling_girl@mail.com

TO: **Ruth Quayle** iamruthquayle@gmail.com

Please don't feel sorry for me! She really isn't a bad mum. She isn't. I know it sounds that way. But you have to know how sorry she is. She could hardly even tell me the story when she got up this morning, but she wouldn't do anything until she'd said it all. She pulled me into her bed with her and made me lie there under her covers and tell her all about you and how you found me and all of it. I just remembered that when I was little, I used to do that, creep in with her. But I hadn't done it in so long! It's funny how I forgot that.

Anyway, she said she'd been awake half the night just turning it over in her head, and she couldn't believe you were alive and that was the miracle, I had to understand that. And then she cried again, and I cried. I'm crying even now while I type this up. There has been so much crying here in the last day that we could cry an entire river for you to be a leaf floating down, if you like. (And I think I almost get what you mean too.)

Then she said, 'Ruby, I want to tell you every single thing, which I was going to tell you when you turned fifteen, because fifteen seemed old enough to handle it. I had a plan. And that's what it was. Fifteen'. Then she cried again and hugged me. I cried too. The sheet was getting soggy because we kept wiping our eyes on it.

She started over. 'I was shattered when your dad died, I was pregnant and alone in New York. I was so young! My heart breaks now for the girl that I was. I was just a girl! And your dad was just a boy! A lovely boy, but just a boy. And then we found out we were having a baby, and it was like we were creating this whole new world. We were prepared to just love you, even though we hadn't any money. We had such romantic ideas. Somehow everything became so big and grand and extravagant when we talked about it, that's how we suddenly got married. We just got swept up'.

She started to cry again. 'But then Philippe died! He DIED. You can't imagine how awful it was, except you can, because of Nan's death. But it was different because it was my HUSBAND and in a foreign country where I never really fit in. I was so lonely. My friends were all just normal starving artists. Young people, who had no idea what to do with the pregnant girl who kept crying because her husband was dead. They didn't even have boyfriends! Not proper ones. They didn't understand about husbands. About how horrid and impossible that was for me'. She looked up at me and said, 'Is this what you want to hear? I'm sorry, darling. It's all so awful and I can't seem to stop crying. You must think I'm mad'.

'A bit', I said. Then I added, 'You've always been a bit mad, Mum. It's OK. I just need you to tell me what happened so I can tell Ruth, do you see'?

'Ruth'! she said. 'I just can't believe she's alive. Can I talk to her? What's her email thingamajig? So I can write her'?

'Mum', I said. 'I don't think she's ready yet. Please keep telling me'.

'It's not too much for you'? she said.

And it was but I shook my head, because I could tell that she'd started now and she was going to keep going anyway, and I knew I had to hear it all, for you. She was crying a little bit again, so I just waited and tried not to cry myself. Then she said, 'When my water broke, I was so scared, I called Nan. Nan and I weren't talking, because she was cross about how Philippe and I had married so quickly.

'So, anyway, I didn't have anyone else. So I called her.

And Nan was such an amazing woman, she managed to get there while I was still in labour. I don't know how she did it. I was in labour for what felt like days! It hurt so much and I was hallucinating. I kept seeing your dad and screaming his name and Nan would say, "He's gone. Concentrate on the babies". And I said, "What BABIES? It's just one baby"!

'I didn't know there were two of you until the moment she said it. I'd had one examination in the very beginning, and that was it. Philippe didn't think much of American doctors, and we couldn't afford regular visits anyway as we didn't have insurance. And I was healthy as an ox for all of my pregnancy, so there wasn't any need. Anyway, the labour wouldn't end, so eventually they had to take you and Ruth out the other way, which was a proper operation. I was out of it with drugs and such, and when I woke up, there you were in the room with me, and I got to hold you, and you were the first miracle.

'Then Nan said, "There's another one". And I said, "Another what"? She said, "Another baby". I thought she'd gone completely off her trolley, just absolutely barking mad. Then I remembered the doctor saying when I arrived at the hospital, "Is it twins"? and that I'd laughed because I'd thought he was joking. They give you laughing gas for the pain, so it all gets mixed up, whether you're laughing because something's funny or because of the gas, and I must have known he wasn't joking. I suddenly understood why I was so huge and why it sometimes felt like there was a whole herd of babies in there, kicking in every direction at once.

'Time did this strange thing then. I can't understand it, so I can't quite explain it, but I expect it was all the drugs. It was like I kept tipping back and forth into dreams that I was desperately trying to wake up from. I don't know how much time passed. When I finally lurched awake, desperate to know what was happening, Nan said, "The second girl won't make it". She was looking at me with this look that she had, it was this really loving look, and I felt like I had when I was a little girl, and she'd take care of things for me. She told me that Ruth's little heart was full of holes, and I should let her go. That I had to let her go. I can't think now why I would have accepted that, except for back then, I was always losing people I loved and I suppose I thought it was happening all over again. I know I screamed. And wailed. And cried.

'I know that I said, "Can I see her"? And Nan said, "No, of course not". And I said, "Give her to me, right now"! She said, "No. Trust me. It's better this way". It just wasn't the English way to do things like that, not like in America and on telly when people are clinging on to their dead babies and howling. I suppose the truth was that she was in the NICU. Of course, I couldn't have held her, she was being kept alive by pumps and wires. But I could have seen her. I just felt so broken. I just wanted Nan to tell me what to do.

I felt like I had completely been torn apart and there was only a thin thread holding me together and Nan held the thread. That was it. She held me together.

'The trouble was . . . well, she was lovely, Nan was, except she was also quite cold. I know you loved her so much that maybe you couldn't see it, the way she was. Efficient, like. A bit . . . removed. I wasn't, though! I was screaming, "GIVE ME THE BABY"! And she was saying, "You can't do that to yourself". And the nurse, I suppose, was saying, "We can take you to her". But Nan was waving her off and saying, "She doesn't want that, respect her wishes". And Nan had a way . . . so I suppose they thought . . . Anyway, I . . .'

She kind of gasped then, and I went and got her some water. My legs were all wobbly. It's a lot to take in about your mum. And your nan. I mean, I really can't think that Nan would do that! That she'd say things like that! I can't quite put it together, not properly, in my head.

After she had some water and cried some more, she kept talking. 'We were in hospital for a few days. I cried and cried. I thought I'd never stop. The nurse said I had the baby blues, that it was a normal thing and it would pass. But it was like my head was full of this haze, and there you were, crying and crying and needing me and needing me, and honestly, I thought I'd get up out of the bed and run away to Brighton, but then I remembered I was in America and you were my daughter, and I couldn't run away. And then I thought of Ruth and cried more and then they put me on some pills so I could stop. It did work! I stopped, but I stopped feeling anything at all. It was the strangest thing. I'd be holding you, and looking at you, and feeding you, and I felt nothing. Like a robot. Like I'd cried out all my insides, and they'd been replaced by steel.

'Nan was pleased. I went along with her because it was the easiest thing. I signed lots of papers and people came and spoke to me but I don't know what they said, I felt like cotton wool was draped all over me, and everything was muffled and far away. I really thought I'd gone mad. I thought they could see that, all of them. I was scared they were going to take YOU. It was terribly confusing. And then there was a lawyer who said, "Are you sure you know that you're giving up this baby for adoption"? And I was so startled. "ADOPTION"? I remember screaming at Nan. And she said that Ruth couldn't be moved to England, she needed too many surgeries, and she was going to die, but there was an American couple who could take care of her until then, better than I could. That the father was a doctor, and it would be the kindest thing. And because I loved Ruth and I was so sick inside and out, I signed the papers.

'And the next thing I knew, Nan said that Ruth was gone and we were heading back home'.

Then she started crying again, that awful crying, the snot rivers, and like she'd never stop. I was so tired, I wanted to curl into her and sleep, and maybe I did a bit. I'm sorry,

Ruth. I was listening to her and trying to take it all in, but it was really hard to hear!

When I woke up, Mum was sitting on the edge of the bed. She said, 'I dream about her, though, every single night. I always dream there are two of you'. Then she said, again, 'It's a miracle'.

I looked around the room and it was all completely the same, the sun spilling in on the white painted floors and the curtains exhaling dust on the sunbeams and the tree outside being all big and green and leafy, and I thought about what you said about the leaf on the river, and I looked at Mum, who was trembling, really like that baby bird on the flypaper, her whole body, even her hair was shaking. And she was waiting for me to say something to make it better, but I didn't know what to say. Finally I said, 'It's OK, Mum'. Then I said, 'It's really Nan who I'm angry with now'.

She laughed in this sad way and then said, 'No, it isn't OK, Ruby. Probably not for Ruth either'.

'No', I managed. 'I suppose not'.

She shook her head. 'And I don't want you to be cross with Nan. She's dead, for one thing. And for another, she was doing what she thought was best. She thought I'd fall apart and not be able to be a mum to either of you. Nan never thought much of my . . . abilities, I suppose you could say. She always thought I'd ruin things and run away. Because I ruined things and ran away a lot when I was young. I wish she'd believed in me. I wish she believed in me like I believe in you'.

'You do'? I said. I was really surprised that she said that. I mean, on top of everything else, I never actually thought she thought I was worth believing in. Not yet, anyway. Maybe when I grew up or that. But not now.

'I do', she said. 'And you know what? I really could do with a tea'.

And then there was no milk. So she went to the shop to get some.

That was about an hour ago.

I said I wasn't going to say I'm sorry again, Ruth, but I am sorry. Are you still coming to England? Please don't be so cross with Mum that you cancel the trip. It's like what you said about being a leaf on the river. I think sometimes it isn't nice at all to be a leaf on the river. Maybe the weather is terrible and cold and there are ducks attacking the leaf, or worse. But I guess the leaf doesn't have any choice. It just floats. And eventually, it gets to the nice bits again, the sun comes out and it's calm and such. I'm probably messing up what you meant in the first place, but that almost makes sense to me.

You don't have to forgive Delilah. You don't have to do anything. You have a mom. Delilah can just be Delilah, this person that you're never going to forgive. But I'll always be your sister.

Love,

Ruby

Ruby to Nan

Dear Nan,

Mum's at the shop buying milk for tea. You know how you always said that tea was the answer, no matter the question? I hope you're right. I don't think you are.

And I definitely don't think you were right about telling Mum to leave Ruth in America. Why did you do that, Nan? I am not feeling frightened right now. I might be alone in the house, but if something goes clunk, I'll know it's you, trying to answer. And if it doesn't go clunk, and you aren't trying to answer, I'm not sure that I can forgive you. I don't think I know how. Even if I am a leaf on the river and everything like that, which made so much more sense when Ruth said it than when I try to. Ruth might forgive you, because of Buddha. BUT I DO NOT.

The letter magnets on the fridge aren't moving. If you don't move those magnets, Nan, I'm just going to end this. I'm going to be furious with you for eternity.

Ruby

Ruth, are you OK?

It's just that you haven't answered. I thought I'd wait and wait and then you'd answer, but you haven't, and I'm panicking. I need you to be OK. I don't know what else to say or to do.

Can you reply? Please?

I'm really worried about Mum. She seems different somehow. Lighter. She's really happy you're alive. She says that even if you don't forgive her, you being alive will always be the best thing that's ever happened in her life. And she's being strange with me, all paying attention, and asking me about my life, and doing other peculiar things. Like she went down to the shops to buy bacon for tea and when she came back, she had forgotten the bacon, but she had got an Alsatian named Peaches. The dog came lolloping into the house like she owned it, weed on the logs by the fireplace, and ate my brand-new plimsolls like they were her very favourite sort of biscuit.

I'm *afraid* of dogs. And likely allergic!

Mum said to me, 'I found an advert for a guard dog on the wall at the shop'.

I felt like I was having a very strange dream. 'What'? I said.

'Ruby', she said. 'I've bollocksed everything up. I'm a terrible mum. I left Ruth in America. I run away when things get hard. Maybe Nan was right to think that I'd not cope. But I . . . well, I'm starting over. I want to make it up to you, and I'm starting by doing all the right things. Nan was on me to get us a dog ages ago, to look after us. And I kept putting it off because I thought we didn't need looking after. But we do. YOU do. This dog is for you, to make up for the fact that I'm a terrible mum. And maybe she can also help us guard the library statue'.

'But Mum'! I said. 'That's completely daft! She's a DOG, not a person! Only a person can be a mum. And you aren't THAT bad. I mean, sometimes you're rubbish, but mostly you're good and you love me and you put food on the table. And the thing about Ruth is that you thought she'd died. That IS pretty terrible, but I'm pretty sure it's Nan's fault, not yours. And I don't think an Alsatian will change anything'!

'I know', she said. 'I just feel so helpless. And somehow when I saw that little sign that said "GUARD DOG FOR SALE", it felt, right then, like the right thing to do'.

Then she burst into tears again. Floods. So did I, because I can't bear to see her sad, and also because I was sad too. It's like we're both mermaids now, but we're swimming around inside a house that's just filled to the brim with sadness instead of water.

We were distracted when Peaches began to gnaw on the table leg quite aggressively. She IS very well trained, though, because when Mum said, 'Oh for goodness' sake, PEACHES', she stopped, and I swear she hung her head in shame. She reeks like a big wool jumper that's been left out in the rain after being sprayed by a cat, and she breathes so heavily, like she is so excited about how she's going to maul her next victim that she can barely bring herself to stop pacing.

Peaches is not just a guard dog, she is a trained *assassin*. All you have to say is 'Harry Potter' and Peaches will kill and eat whoever is in the room. The code words to stop her in her tracks are 'Hermione Granger', so I have been walking about muttering 'Hermione Granger' because I don't want Peaches to get confused. She has enormous teeth and the facial expression of someone who got left behind twice in Year Three and is more than a little narked about it.

There's still so much to talk about with Mum, but Peaches takes up all the room in this house with her smells and sounds and general terrifying-ness! I'm sure your Caleb is lovely, but I can't help but look at dogs and think they are all just looking back at me like I'm some sort of walking, talking, trembling meat.

Ruth, are you OK? Are you being a leaf on the river? I just need to know that you're all right. That you're going to forgive her or maybe just try, that this is all going to be OK.

I love you. And we're sisters forever, no matter what.

Even if you decide you can't do it, be the leaf, forgive Delilah, any of that. You don't have to. It doesn't change us.

Does it?

Ruby

FROM: **Ruby Starling** starling_girl@mail.com

TO: **Fiona** fififionafifi@aol.co.uk

Mum's bought a dog. A DOG, FI. What am I supposed to do with an Alsatian? I've *never* liked dogs, *everyone* knows that. This one also is a trained killer. I don't think that makes it better.

I'm attaching the emails I just sent to Ruth because my wrists are sore from typing and I can't say all that again. She hasn't replied yet and I'm terribly worried but I don't know what to do about it. She's never given me her number or anything! So I can't call her. Anyway, phones make me nervous! Why hasn't she replied? I know it's a lot to take in. I just need to know she's OK.

You forgot the attachment! What's happened? Shall I come round?

Alsatians are my favourite. They're so smart, you know. And fashionable. I read in the rags that Madonna has got three to guard her estate.

More importantly, BERK IS HERE. You're *definitely* going to fancy him, Ru. I know you say you won't, but he's the spitting image of Nate! He's even got that awful emo hair! I burst out laughing when I saw him. But it's like he was made for you. Want to come round to mine and meet him? PLEASE?

I'll try the attachment again.

Oh, also, Fi, it's super important that you tell everyone in your family not to say 'Harry Potter' in front of Peaches. She's actually trained to kill if you say those words. I'd best never take her to Waterstones. Don't come round. Mum's having a bath and a think. I'll come to you. Read the attachment so we can talk about it when I get there. I can't say it all out loud. It's easier just to read it, Fi. Trust me. It's just . . . a lot.

FROM: **Delilah Starling** theartistdelilah@yahoo.co.uk

TO: **Ruby Starling** starling_girl@mail.com

Ruby, I know you're at Fi's, but I was just thinking that the most important thing here is this miracle we've received: She's alive! Your sister is alive! It's all so shivery and strange, like a shimmering oasis in a desert.

I'm not sure what to do. Or say. Or what happens next. A proper mum would probably know. Which is how I know I'm letting you down again. I'm sorry, Ruby. I really am.

I know that I said before that I thought dead people don't have wishes that they needed to have fulfilled after they are dead, but I was wrong about that, I've decided. I think Nan wanted this to happen.

I'm working out what to say to Ruth. Tell me when she replies to you. Tell me if she's ready.

Love,
Mum

Ruby to Nan

Dear Nan,

I'd given up mostly. I walked around the house and all the paintings were still hanging perfectly and the magnets on the fridge didn't shift. There weren't any crashes and nothing happened. The only noises were from the large, smelly dog that Mum brought home. Peaches is her name, but I know you know that, if you're real, but you aren't. That's the confusing bit. Because, Nan, just when I was convinced I'd made the whole thing up, Peaches brought me the boot. My blue suede boot! With your letter in it.

Your letter, Nan! I don't know how you did it, how you got Peaches to find it and bring it to me, but it was brilliant. At first, I was furious of course. I thought she was eating my boot, not delivering your note. When I realized, I gave her a whole block of cheese. She loves cheese.

I'm a bit scared to read the letter. Silly, I know. I'll do it now, though. I just wanted to write to you first to say that I believe you're here, after all.

Hi Nan. I love you and miss you so much!

I said that out loud. Did you hear?

Love,

Ruby

Ed,

Sorry, this isn't a real note. I don't know what to say to you. I do believe in ghosts, though. I thought you should know. I really do.

Ruby

Nan to Ruby (handwritten on blue paper)

Dearest, darling Ruby,

If you are reading this, it means I have passed on (passed up?) to that great next step, whatever it might be. Don't be sad. I hope you are a teenager, at least, and can cope, but as I am writing this letter, you are only 11. You are so much like your mum at your age, it's uncanny. Sometimes I almost call you `Delilah' by mistake, seeing your head bent over your drawing or the way you push your hair behind your ear.

I just hope you aren't EXACTLY like her, not in all her ways. Did I ever tell you about all the times she ran away from home as a teenager? We used to have a detective who we dealt with exclusively when she did another runner. He'd always track her down. It started off with big things, but eventually she did it for everything. When she did badly on her o-levels, when her dad was cross with her for burning the tea, when a boy she liked didn't call her when she hoped he would. She was a bit mad, I suppose. We loved her, but she was always like a bird, always flying off somewhere.

When you were born, you were loveliness embodied. Oh, I could have eaten you up! You were perfect. I know it's not very properly grandmotherly of me to say those things, I should teach you to keep your emotions in check, but I still feel amazed—almost like crying—when I look at you. You are still amazing, even if you don't feel it because you have spots or lank hair or you are in love with the wrong person or whatever dreadful teenage affliction is plaguing you. I hope if I teach you anything, it's that you don't need a man (or a boy) to give you an identity. You are you and you are unbearably perfect regardless of whether the boy you have a crush on likes you back or the other girls in your class tease you because you're different and cleverer than most. Your mum got teased a lot.

This is the part in the letter where I tell you what I know. What I did, really.

And what I know is this: You were born a twin, and

your twin is dead. Her name — unless they changed it — was Ruth Elizabeth. She was born with a heart condition, the poor little love. Full of holes, it was.

I was so afraid she'd leave you both, I did the only thing I could do. I lied. I never lie. I know that your mum has her issues with me, but believe me when I say this was the only time I lied to her, outright. I know that I did the right thing, telling her that Ruth was dead, when she wasn't. Not then. I actually let her be adopted, knowing that she wouldn't survive a week. It was all so American and legal and there were lawyers and it was overwhelming, even for me, but I had to be strong. I had to be strong for both your mum and myself. I had to make decisions. I didn't know it was going to be like how it was, with all those people and social workers and interviews. But the more I said it, the more firmly I believed it. Your mum wasn't competent enough to cope with two of you, if one of you was dying. That poor baby would have to be in the hospital for her whole life, however long it would be, not dead but not exactly alive either. Your mum, she couldn't have coped. She just couldn't.

And maybe I couldn't either. There. I said it. I didn't know how to look after a baby so frail. I didn't know what to do for that angel except let her go.

I know it sounds heartless. I know it felt heartless. But it was impossible for your mum. She was barely hanging on after Philippe went. I had to get her back to

England. America was breaking her heart, which was already broken. She was like a bird that couldn't fly, do you see? She needed to come home where I could help her properly, at her own home, in her own bed, with you by her side. You were her baby, but she was mine.

Everyone just does the best they can. That's the thing of it. That's all we can ever do.

I just wanted you to know, suddenly. In case your mum never told you. She always said that she would, when you were ready, but I don't know if she'll ever believe you are. I don't think she feels ready for it herself, to tell you that there was Ruth once, and now there isn't. That you were once a sister. I just got this idea that maybe you'd feel somehow like there was a piece missing and I wanted to tell you that yes, there is. One missing, beautiful piece.

I love you so much, darling girl. I love you for always. And I'm terribly sorry to have died, which I must have done, or you wouldn't be reading this at all, would you?

Love you, my girl.

Nan

FROM: **Ruby Starling** starling_girl@mail.com

TO: **Ruth Quayle** iamruthquayle@gmail.com

Ruth,
I know that sorry isn't enough. What can I do? I have so much to say, but I can't say it until I know you're OK. Until I know you're there.
Ruby

FROM: **David Quayle** docdaddave@gmail.com

TO: **Ruth Quayle** iamruthquayle@gmail.com

Ruth, *please* walk Caleb. Mommy and I are at the restaurant now. I wish you'd come with us! Are you sure you're OK? I'll bring you a dessert.
Love,
Daddy
Sent from my iPhone

DAD, for goodness' sake, it's DAD, not DADDY!

I am so close to 13 now, it's like I'm practically inhaling the same oxygen as I will be breathing on my 13th birthday! When I am a teenager, will you believe that I no longer should call you DADDY?

I'm sorry, I'm fine. I mean, I'll probably be OK. You know what the calendar said today? "All wrongdoing arises because of mind. If mind is transformed, can wrongdoing remain?" Well, I guess I need to transform my mind from the leaf to the river or the foot to the path or whatever you think makes the most sense, but I have to forgive Delilah Starling before I get broken inside. Because that could totes happen. I can already feel it happening. It's like something is curling up and turning black and it's scary, Dad. I don't like it. But I know I can do it! I can figure this out. I feel like maybe I already have, actually. It just took me a few days.

I'll tell you about it all later, OK? But don't worry about it. I'm absolutely fine and anyway, Jedgar is here and we are doing stuff for our movie. Did you know that Delilah Starling has a whole big book of art, which we checked out of the library? She's done about a million paintings of me and Ruby. What if I'd just found this book one day while I was spelunking through the library shelves aimlessly? I might have dropped dead of a heart attack on the spot. I don't think Ashley Mary Jane's heart could have coped with it at all.

Stop looking at your iPhone! Pay attention to Mom! Tell her that her hair looks nice!

Love,
Ruth

FROM: **Ruth Quayle**   iamruthquayle@gmail.com

TO: **Gen Quayle**   Gen@usdinolab.org

Mom,

You looked really, really nice tonight. I just wanted to say that! You look amazing! No one would ever guess your age! And Dad is lucky to be married to you, and I bet he thinks so too, even if he forgets to say things like, "Wow, those shoes make your legs look amazeballs!"

And you're a really really good mom. I don't think I remember to tell you THANK YOU for being so awesome all the time, but I'm lucky and I love you and all that. More than . . . well, more than anything.

Love,
Ruth

The thing is that
someone always wants
the runt.
The runts sell first.
A family comes and
the kids always say,
"That one." And point
to the smallest one.
They want to save it.
I did.

And so you were saved.
And thrived.
And so?
Now what?

There are things you
have to say.
Woof, you say,
your bark strong and hearty,
like you can hardly remember
anyway, how you were once
the smallest,
the most wanted.

Dear Ruby,

Dad says that Buddha says, "You will not be punished for your anger, you will be punished by your anger." It's what I mean about how I *have* to forgive your mom. Being mad at her has been this *thing* I've been carrying around basically forever. It hasn't done anything but made me tired from carrying it. So now I'm going to put it down. Which is sort of easy, I know that. But also sort of not. Because you can say a thing like, "Oh, I forgive you!" and expect you'll be lighter, but the thing is that you have to really really really mean it, I think, for it to work. So it lets you go. I'm trying, but it feels like a lie.

It's just easier to be mad, I guess.

Tell her she can write to me, please?

Yes! We are still coming. I seriously cannot wait to meet you.

Ruth

Dear Nan,

I love you.

You were a wonderful nan even if what you did was pretty terrible. I'm sad that you'll never meet Ruth and she'll never meet you.

And I'm angry.

I've never felt like this before, like I want to go all the way down to the cemetery and graffiti your headstone. Or kick it over.

I can't believe you thought that was the right thing to do! Why couldn't you have believed in Mum, just a little bit? Would that have been so bad?

Because I could have known Ruth forever. We could have been mates at school. We could have had each other. A proper sister. A best friend.

And Nan, I feel like you took that away. Because you didn't trust that Mum could cope. And she could have, Nan. Maybe not like YOU would've done it, but I believe in her. She's scatty and mad and sometimes completely barmy, but she's got a heart full of love.

I don't know if I can forgive you. And you being dead complicates that an awful lot. I don't know how to be angry with someone who is dead. Do I shout at rainbows now? Is that how it will be? I'm not going to write again. Maybe not ever. Ruth might be able to figure all of this out. She's practically Buddhist! So she can put down the heavy bit she's been carrying around! Because it makes sense to her! But it doesn't make sense to me. And I don't think I can, Nan.

I don't know if I want to.

Ruby

FROM: Chlophie!!! chlophie@hotmail.co.uk

TO: Ruby Starling starling_girl@mail.com ;
Fiona fififionafifi@aol.co.uk

Don't forget that Sophie's do is a surprise! Don't include us in your e's about it because then you'll wreck everything! I've invented a new email addy for this, which is justchloealone @hotmail.co.uk. Can you use that?

Chloe

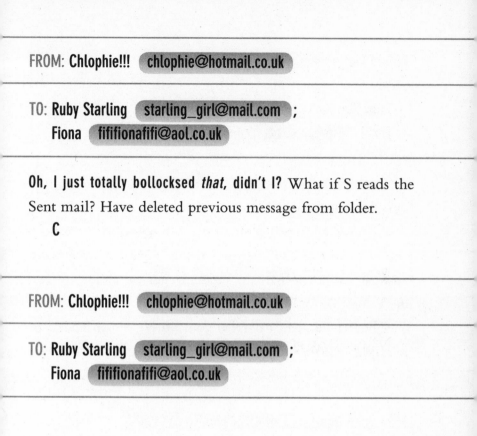

FROM: Chlophie!!! chlophie@hotmail.co.uk

TO: Ruby Starling starling_girl@mail.com ;
Fiona fififionafifi@aol.co.uk

Oh, I just totally bollocksed *that*, didn't I? What if S reads the
Sent mail? Have deleted previous message from folder.
   C

FROM: Chlophie!!! chlophie@hotmail.co.uk

TO: Ruby Starling starling_girl@mail.com ;
Fiona fififionafifi@aol.co.uk

Never mind, she's just messaged me to say that she didn't see
anything about the surprise, after all! From now on, I'll
ONLY use the new email! Phew! Relief!
   C

I just did it again, didn't I?

I'm making a real hash of everything. But we've been Chlophie forever and ever, practically since we were born! Gosh, it would be hard to suddenly *just* be Chloe, in real life. I don't think I could do that.

Oh, Ru-Ru, can I borrow your purple dress? That'd be smashing.

Dear Mom and Dad,

~~I am writing you this letter because~~

~~I would like to talk to you about~~

~~Please excuse the fact I am writing to you instead of talking to you~~

~~I'm sorry, but I~~

Hi guys!

I've printed out Ruby's last email for you to read. You should probably read it sitting down and with tissues, because it's sad. I have nothing else to say about it but you should read it, so you know, before we go to England. It's important.

I know we didn't get a chance to talk much when you got home from dinner the other day, and then you were both so busy at work, I didn't want to bug you. (By the way, Caleb had a huge bulging tick in his ear and I dug it out with tweezers and left it on your bathroom counter so you could see how disgusting it was and be proud of me for getting it out without barfing. He's fine now.)

I love you and I'm sorry if this makes you sad (not the tick, but the email).

I am not mad at Delilah anymore. I thought you should know that. She's just a person. Jedgar said something a long time ago about how none of this changes me, and you know what? He's both completely wrong and completely right. It doesn't change OUR family. It changes me in some ways, but not in important ones. I am still me. And I'm OK.

Love,
Ruth

FROM: **Ruth Quayle** `iamruthquayle@gmail.com`

TO: **Jedgar Allen Johnston** `JedgarAllenPoe@yahoo.com`

I've just realized how it has to end. Not *SHORCA!* But the documentary.

FROM: **Jedgar Allen Johnston** `JedgarAllenPoe@yahoo.com`

TO: **Ruth Quayle** `iamruthquayle@gmail.com` ·

OK. How?

FROM: **Ruth Quayle** `iamruthquayle@gmail.com`

TO: **Jedgar Allen Johnston** `JedgarAllenPoe@yahoo.com`

I have to forgive her, I guess. Because I'm a leaf on the river and she's a leaf on the river and that's all of us, just floating down the river.

All I need is for Delilah to say "Sorry." Just to say it.
And then I THINK I can forgive her. I'll do it.

Then that's the end, do you see? It just ends with that.

FROM: **Jedgar Allen Johnston**   JedgarAllenPoe@yahoo.com

TO: **Ruth Quayle**   iamruthquayle@gmail.com

I think I get it now, why you were acting so weird about
Freddie Blue Anderson and flipping out and stuff. It's like
you said, like your own river suddenly turned into Victoria
Falls. I wasn't like-LIKING Freddie Blue anyway. You can
talk to a girl without like-liking them, you know. You
can even be friends. We're friends. (And don't you dare start
talking about that thing that happened earlier this summer.
That was a lifetime ago.) Anyway, you're right about the
ending. I'm working on *SHORCA!* now that it makes sense.
I can't sleep. It's 4:00 in the morning and I've been working
on it all night. It's like I can't think about anything else but
making it awesome, which is good, because it saves me from
thinking about how my brothers are idiots or about how
you went sort of crazy there for a while with that contract
and weirdness about FBA, who I don't actually like-like
at all.

I'm not going to show this to you until it's totally done. You're going to love me. I mean, *it*. You're going to love *SHORCA!* (Well, it AND me. Ha ha, j/k.) When you get back from England, you can teach me some more of your Buddha stuff. I feel like I might need to get how I'm a leaf on the river and a river with a leaf on it next time Spike switches my lunch out for a dog food sandwich. We don't even have a dog.

It would be a lot easier to be a river than to be me sometimes, I think.

J.

Ruby to Nan

Dear Nan,

I'm sorry. I didn't really mean that.
　　Love,
　　Ruby

Mum,

I took Peaches for a walk just now. We walked all the way into town and stopped by the library to visit the sculpture of me. I like it a lot better without that box round it. The box was horrid.

Anyway, I tied Peaches up and darted into Starbucks for a cocoa, and when I came out, there was someone just standing there with a tin of paint! Before I could even react, Peaches let out this terrifying growl, somehow untied herself from the post where I'd knotted her leash, and leapt forwards. She was like an animal on a nature programme! A lion leaping on a poor, sick antelope! I didn't even have to SAY 'Harry Potter'! She just knew what to do, like she'd been waiting her whole life for exactly this. I didn't get a look at who it was, because lucky for him, he ran fast.

Mum, do you remember that it's only two more days till Ruth comes? Did you write her yet? Because you sort of have to. You have to say something before she's just HERE in our front room with us.

Love,

Ruby

Of course. I'm writing to her now. You run along to Sophie's do and try to put all this on the back burner, at least for a few hours. Have a smashing time! Can you take Peaches? It's lovely how the two of you have bonded, and the trainer said that you should try to do everything together for a while, to cement that bond. Do you think she might just lie down quietly in a corner somewhere and not bother anyone?

You know, darling, I think buying Peaches for you is maybe one of the things I did right, after all.

Love,
Mummy

Dear Ruth,
I'm sorry. I know that's not enough, but it's my starting point. Ruby says you're a poet. I don't know what to say or

even what I feel, or, goodness knows, what you feel, but I
wrote you this.

Two babies, they said.
I held one girl:
pink faced and bawling,
daughtering me.
The other was just an idea.
Nothing to do with
this.
Everything to do with
this.
Blue, they said,
the other one is
the palest blue.
I saw a winter sky,
fading blue to grey
with cold.
The pink girl
screamed, hot
and livid in my
arms.
Inside
me
something
broke

or froze
and I didn't
hold on to what
was mine.
I didn't know how
to be what I wasn't:
Mother
to anyone.

That's what I wrote, for you. It's terrible, isn't it? But I mean it. Poetry is always falling away from me. I think it sounds right, exactly like what I want to say, but it never quite comes out how I mean it. At the same time, I don't know how to say what I want to say any other way.

I am sorry. Maybe I should have just said that and nothing else, but it doesn't seem like enough.

I can't wait to meet you.

Love,

Your Mother

OK, I said that I could forgive her if she said sorry, and she did. I have a note in my email from my very own actual biological mother and it says sorry.

But I don't forgive her.

I am still mad!

I thought I would stop being mad and forgive her and be peaceful and in the moment and life is suffering and the sky is not the way, the heart is the way, and ALL THAT BUD-DHIST STUFF would MAKE SENSE, but it turns out that I'm still feeling totes angry and hurt!

And I think her poem is terrible.

I don't even want to reply.

FROM: **Ruby Starling** starling_girl@mail.com

TO: **Ruth Quayle** iamruthquayle@gmail.com

Ruth,

It's the middle of the night. It must be day there. I've just got back from Sophie's birthday bash.

Mum's asleep. I checked on her right away. Her cheeks were all blotchy, like she'd had a cry, and the laptop was open next to her with the screen saver on. Did she write to you? What did she say? Is everything OK? You're still coming, right?

The party was amazeog, which is Chlophie's word, which I always thought was silly, but completely fits this party, because it was their party, so it WAS amazeog! It was really too bad that you weren't here today instead of Tuesday. You'd have loved it! And you could have met everyone. Soph's mum had set up this cinema screen in the back garden, where she played some fab films. There were cakes all done up in white (everything was white) and music and silly games like we played when we were little, and a bouncy castle even. Anyone else would have been like, 'Oh Mum, for goodness' sake, I'm 15 now', but Chloe and Sophie thought it was the best thing ever, and so everyone went along with it and it was brill.

The whole night, Chloe kept whispering instructions on how she was going to get even with Hawkster and Angus, but it was terrifically complicated and Fi and I had no idea what she was talking about. It never would have worked, her plan! But luckily, it didn't have to, because of Peaches.

I had Peaches with me, and all evening, she'd been just lying in the corner, licking her feet, a bit like a really large and frightening cat. People stayed clear of her because she doesn't look very friendly. Anyway, I was standing at the back, near where Hawkster and Angus were having this fight about whether Harry Potter was a total wazzock or not.

HARRY POTTER.

Well, Peaches leapt right over the table when she heard that name, and Angus yelled, 'Oi! Run for it! It's that mad dog again! He's out to get me! He's been chasin' me all afternoon'!

So I grabbed Peaches's collar and said, 'Oh, so *you* were vandalising my mum's art in the library square'? Peaches was vibrating, she wanted to get to him so badly. I whispered 'Hermione Granger' so that he couldn't hear. Can't have him knowing the code, but Peaches is smart. She kept growling then let out this most ferocious bark. Made my hair stand up too.

Well, Angus turned purple in the face and set off at a dead sprint, with Hawkster right behind. I shouted after him, 'Don't go near that statue again'! I'm pretty sure he won't. Then both Angus and Hawkster fell into the decorative koi pond when they tried to run across the Japanese bridge! Splashing around like they were drowning, even though the water didn't go past their knees! Everyone was killing themselves laughing.

Peaches looked very proud of herself, so I gave her an entire piece of cake. She deserved it.

Oh, did I tell you that Fi's got a sort-of-almost-cousin staying with her? His name is Berk and he looks an awful lot like Nate from STOP, who I just stopped being in love with, just at the party just now. The minute I saw Berk, my stomach felt funny and my face went red. Fi whispered, 'I knew you'd fancy him'! And I think I might!

It's silly, I know. I'm not even 13. But when I came home, I was going to sit down and listen to some STOP like I always used to do when I couldn't sleep, but it's like whatever I felt for Nate? That wasn't love at all! And it just flew out of the room, on the feathers of an invisible bird, swooping out the door, never to be seen again.

I just thought I'd tell you.

I am really excited to see you in two days.

Two days, Ruth! Can you even believe it?

WRITE BACK RIGHT AWAY, RUTH QUAYLE.

Love,

Ruby

nopoppingballoons.tumblr.com

Not knowing how to feel is like how once,
you went to cross the river and the stones were slippery
and you fell in and the water was at first so cold
you thought you would drown
because no air came
but you didn't.
You stayed in the water for hours, playing,

until your lips turned blue and your mom made
you come out and your dad built a little fire on the
riverbank to warm you up.
It's like you want to know everything about everything
and find things out
and know who you are
but at the same time,
you kind of want s'mores
and for your parents to wrap a blanket
around you and tell you stories like you are
just a kid,
still.
But the next day you try again
and this time you get across the river
and you find out things you didn't know
you wanted to know
and when you get back to your parents
you are someone different,
after all because
as it turns out
you *are* the river.

Ruby,

I am so super happy for you that your party was fun and that you met a boy! That's great!

Except I'm not really that happy, Ruby. I'm not. I feel mean and like I don't want to be happy for you, but then I don't know why I want to be mean to you, but I do, so maybe I shouldn't write you this email. Maybe I shouldn't say anything at all. But I don't know how you can go to a party and talk to a cute boy and do normal, fun things when I'm way over here and your mom wrote me a poem that I don't really understand and it's twisted my insides up like a fishtail hair braid. It's like I get that it's beautiful but it isn't what I wanted her to say, but I don't know what I wanted her to say, and I don't know how that's like hair either, so don't ask. I thought I would forgive her, like Buddha, if she said sorry, but I still don't feel it! Not really! I still feel all heavy and confused and MAD!

I don't even want to come. Not anymore. But Mom says that I have to. She says I'll regret it if I don't. But I don't know if I will regret it! I might regret coming. Because I might say something awful to you or to your mom, because I might be a bad person inside. All this time I've been thinking I was a good type of person who could see the good in everyone (except maybe Freddie Blue Anderson), but actually, I'm not. This whole time, I've been like a lava flow of red-hot anger, just waiting to bubble up and scald everyone I touch. I'm not Buddhist and peaceful and forgiving and flowing like a river or a leaf or a path or anything, I'm just a regular kid who can't figure out how not to be sad about all of this forever.

SHE GAVE ME AWAY.

I was going to use that part about lava in a poem but now I won't bother. You're probably the only one who reads my Tumblr anyway.

Love,

Ruth

FROM: **Ruth Quayle** iamruthquayle@gmail.com

TO: **Ruby Starling** starling_girl@mail.com

Ruby,

I'm sorry. Ignore my last note completely. Delete it if you haven't already and never read it again. I'm just mixed up! I don't know how to feel. Not really. One minute I THINK that I know, and then the next minute, I realize that I'm just completely wrong about all of it.

Anyway, there's another secret.

Sometimes when I can't sleep, I go out onto the roof and I lie on my back and look up at the stars. Me and Mom used to lie there for ages and then Dad would come up and point out all the proper names for the constellations and Mom would tease him about being so literal about everything and not being able to imagine what else might be there. So tonight I was lying there and the stars were really amazeballs, and I thought, *I should go get Mom and Dad! And we can all lie up here together, like we used to when I was smaller! And it will be great, like old times before any of this happened!*

So I scooted across the roof — which is flat, it's not like I was scaling a slippery peak — and jumped down onto Mom and Dad's balcony. I could hear them talking and I was just about to knock and surprise them when I heard the words "DO NOT TELL RUTH."

I froze. What were they talking about? What secrets did they have? Because we had promised that there would not be any secrets and yet there I was, in the middle of the night outside their window, and they were talking about SECRETS.

Then Caleb began barking like a lunatic at the bottom of the trellis and attempting to climb his way up to me! *Zut alors!* Luckily, Dad just went down and let Caleb inside. Then he went back to the bedroom where I was finally able to hear the following conversation:

Dad: She's obviously forgotten, and if we miss it, is it really that big of a deal? We couldn't have known it was the same date. I mean, we should have known. Oh, the letter from the agency came! Of course, it doesn't say anything, except that the adoption was closed. Remember when that woman sneezed into my coffee?

Mom: I . . . guess. [*mumble mumble*] We should sue them! Or not. No. Not. I don't have the energy for that, and besides, what would we sue them for?

Dad: I *know* how they feel. This is terrible. [*mumble*]

Mom: But how will Ruth feel? Maybe we should leave it up to her. Her choice. You do NOT know what it's like to be a thirteen-year-old kid in this situation . . . It might be important to her.

Dad: She's my daughter. Of course I know what she's feeling. AND A-HA! You just did it too!

Mom: Did what?

Dad: She's only TWELVE, remember? Rounder-upper!

Mom: I am not a rounder-upper! Besides, David, that isn't the point, is it?

Dad: What IS the point, Gen?

Mom: Oh, I don't know. I don't know anything. Why is everything happening at once? It's like our lives are a giant pinball machine and we are zinging around inside it.

Dad: If your job ends, does this mean we can move Luffetta out of the dining room? I always hated that thing.

She gives me bad dreams! I'd never admit that to Ruth, though, remember when she . . . [*mumble*] [*hearty laughter*]

Mom: DAVID. That's not funny. Luffetta is practically family.

Which is when I blurted out, "EXACTLY! AND FAMILY IS NOT DISPOSABLE!"

Dad *flung* the window open, which unfortunately knocked me directly in the face, possibly breaking my nose, which began to gush with blood. (I take aspirin every day, so I bleed more than normal people do. It's totes dramatic!)

"What are you DOING, Ruth?" he said.

"I was . . . ," I said. "Nothing."

They both just stared at me like I'd grown flippers and announced I was a mermaid. Finally Mom said, "Your nose! David, do something!"

So Dad brought me into their bedroom and got out his doctor bag and put this powdery stuff inside my nose that made it stop bleeding. It also smells like mustard. It's really terrible. There was a lot of rushing around. When it finally ended, I was exhausted. I mean, I didn't want to go look at constellations anymore. I just wanted to go to bed.

"Well, good night!" I said. I tried to walk away proudly and swiftly, without mentioning the so-called secrets that I overheard when I was innocently hanging outside their window. Unfortunately, when I moved, my nose started up again in a torrential downpour of blood.

Mom and Dad whisked me to the hospital and bought me a stuffed cat and a chocolate bar in the gift shop. As though I can be bought off with stuffies and candy, which, as it turns out, I actually can, so that was nice! The only thing on the television in the waiting area was *SpongeBob SquarePants,* which is basically an insult to all humans everywhere. (He's a KITCHEN SPONGE!) Luckily, when you are bleeding a lot, they hurry you through and before I knew it, I was in the little curtained-off area and Dad's friend Dr. Mike was cauterizing my nose. If this has never happened to you, AVOID. It sizzles. Like a tiny little barbecue in your nostril.

I'm so sleepy, Ruby. Plus, my nose is throbbing like a bullfrog singing to the full moon.

And now that everyone is in bed, I've just realized I still don't know what Mom and Dad were talking about. What do I need to decide? What are they keeping from me? Can't anyone just tell me the truth? EVER?

Love,
Ruth

Mum,

I'm scared. And I don't really know why. I'm scared all over, like every bit of me is just waiting to fall from something terrifyingly high, like the Shard building or the Cliffs of Dover.

What if she doesn't like me? What if she can't forgive you? What if she takes one look at us and runs away?

Love,

Ruby

It's not long now, Fi. Only a day. I don't know what to do. I'm so restless, but I can't seem to go out or do anything, so I'm just sitting here in the wardrobe, thinking and listening to STOP, or trying to. It's just that maybe I don't really like them anymore. You know, Berk REALLY does look like Nate. Only a bit better. Did he say anything about me?

I KNEW it! Oh, this is the best! Shall I tell him? Or d'you want to? Or should we just let it play out however it's going to? It's so *romantic*! I'm so happy.

I know you're scared about Ruth, but it's going to be fine. I promise it will be fine. Besides, it'll be even stranger for her, I'd think. It's YOUR mum. And YOU.

I was reading one of Dad's true crimes last night, and it was about a girl who was kidnapped and stored in a shed out back of some creepy stalker's house for ten whole years, and then when she came out, all she wanted was to see all her old school chums, but of course they were all different by then, all grown up and such. And she was so shocked. So maybe — I know it's completely different, obvi — Ruth will just want to see what she's missed? You should get out your old photo albums, so you can show her. And . . . oh, you'll know what to do. You'll know when you see her.

Can I come round and meet her? Not right away, but maybe an hour in? Or for tea?

FROM: **Ruby Starling** starling_girl@mail.com

TO: **Fiona** fififionafifi@aol.co.uk

Of course!

FROM: **Chlophie!!!** chlophie@hotmail.co.uk

TO: **Ruby Starling** starling_girl@mail.com

Ru-Ru, we've just heard that Fi's meeting your glam American twin. 'Course you don't want us hanging round too, but on the off chance that you're bored or need a laugh, we're not doing anything except dyeing our hair with blueberries and a turnip. Apparently it makes a smashing hair dye! Who knew? Soph says not turnip, but beetroot. OK, well, blueberries and BEETROOT then. Stop doing that while I'm typing, Soph! This is important! Ruby's going to meet her twin! Gosh, I wish something so exciting would happen to us.

Kiss kiss, one on each cheek, like *le français*!

Chloe and Sophie (Even though, once again, Soph didn't even bend a finger to type a single letter, lazy cow.)

COME DOWNSTAIRS RIGHT NOW. (We have ice cream sandwiches!)

Also, while you're down here, there's something your mom and I need to talk to you about. Don't panic. It's nothing major. Just a little . . . something. Something you need to know before the cab gets here.

Oh, by the way, on the calendar today, Buddha says, "You, yourself, as much as anybody in the entire universe, deserve your love and affection." Something to think about, sweetie. I mean, if you don't forgive anyone, then you aren't exactly being loving to yourself either, are you? It might go back to the idea that you can't forgive someone else until you forgive yourself. Maybe you can't forgive yourself for surviving, after all, and causing all this? Because if that's what you're thinking, you're wrong. You surviving all this was the best thing that happened to any of us. Ever. Not kidding.

And get down here! I'm going to eat your ice cream!

Love,

Daddy

j/k! I meant "Dad."

I'm coming!

DO NOT LET CALEB SLATHER ALL OVER MY DESSERT.

Why are we having dessert for breakfast? Won't we get type 2 diabetes? Can I also have some fruit or something? I don't want to throw up on the plane!

Love,

Ruth

P.S. I am so, so nervous.

P.P.S. Mom, are you sure you are OK with all of this?

P.P.P.S. All this Buddhist stuff may be too much for me. I know it works for you but you've read books! You have this huge understanding! The page-a-day calendar doesn't cut it, Dad. I sort of still don't get HOW you let go, just that you have to do it. I will say it here officially: "I, Ruth Quayle, forgive myself." There.

I just want it to be true. What does Buddha say about that?

Sweetie, I am completely fine. I'm desperately worried about how YOU are coping, but I'm looking forward to the twelve hours of flying so that you and I can really talk. We'll be fine. This will be fine. I think it's good for you. It's like you've got this huge, extended family now, not just us. You've got the McNays and now you've got Ruby and her mom.

And your dad is right about the forgiving. Maybe you feel guilty that you survived, but maybe you also feel guilty for having Ashley's heart? Your psychiatrist said this might be something you deal with around this age, this idea that you survived at the cost of her. It's OK, Ruth. I promise, it's OK. Whatever you're feeling is OK. And forgiving yourself is OK too. Not just in words, but for real.

Oh, speaking of the McNays, can you *please* come down? That's what we have to talk about.

Love,
Mommy

I'm in ENGLAND! Can you even believe this?

This is crazy! We are just checking into the hotel and there is Internet, so I wanted to write to you RIGHT AWAY. You know, for your documentary. I kind of sort of wish you were here, filming it, but you aren't and that's fine too! I have a camera! I will get footage!

I've just watched *SHORCA!* and Jedgar, it is the best thing you've ever done! When I was making those little clay shark/orca hybrids, I didn't know that you could do THAT kind of magic computer stuff. Your drawings are amazing. And at the end, when the SHORCA realizes there is another SHORCA and stops chomping the beach-goers and swims off into the sunset while the voice-over says, "LIKE ALL MAMMALS, SHORCAS CRAVE THE COMPANIONSHIP OF ONE OF THEIR OWN KIND" . . . well, it actually made my eyes well up and then spill over, all over my cheeks in a giant flood of weeping.

It's different here. Even the air feels different, like it has more gray in it and it's all a little foggy and serious.

This is actually really happening.

I'm not going to know what to say.

Jedgar, I wish I hadn't come.

Ruth

FROM: **Jedgar Allen Johnston** JedgarAllenPoe@yahoo.com

TO: **Ruth Quayle** iamruthquayle@gmail.com

What? You don't *really* wish that.

You had to go there. You have to meet Ruby. She's your twin sister!

And you pretty much have to meet your biological mom too. It's going to be OK, Ruth.

You'll totally know the right thing to say when you see her. Or when you see *them*, I mean. I mean, think about it. What's the worst that can happen?

No, scratch that. *Don't* think about that. You're a river, remember? A pretty crazy river with lots of weird twists and turns, but still just a river.

And a leaf.

Jedgar

P.S. Thanks for saying all that stuff about *SHORCA!* I think it's pretty good too. It's already got 112 hits on You-Tube and only half of them were me.

Best. Day. Ever.

Even if it was the saddest. It was also the best.

And the strangest.

Because you do look EXACTLY like me. I guess I thought you'd be a bit different.

Anyway, it was really lovely. I'm crying now because I don't want you to go, but I know you'll have to go. You only have these few days.

Maybe I will go to uni in America! They have fashion there too. Really fab fashion.

Miss you already,

Ruby

J.,

Attached is the video that I took today. I think it's the
ending of the documentary, even if you haven't finished the
beginning or the middle yet. Or even if you never do.

We are all real people and the video shows what really
happened. It was awkward like it looks, but even when you
watch it, Jedgar, you can't know what it was like! It was
amazingly, gloriously, wonderfully, unbelievably, totally,
completely the strangest thing that's ever happened to anyone. When I saw Ruby for the first time, it was like I just
fell out of myself and into her, and for the first few seconds,
it was like we were the same person. That sounds totes crazy
to you. I know it does, because it sounds entirely crazy to
me too, and I'm the one it happened to. I was bawling and
so was she and right behind her was Delilah and she was
crying too. (Everyone was. It was like that. Well, you can
see that, you don't need me to tell you!)

You know, this whole time, when I was at home and
Googling Delilah and being mad about being the runt that
she shoved out of the way so that Ruby could be strong,
I thought that Delilah was going to be bigger. Then when I
saw her, her hands were shaking and she kept tying her long

273

hair into a knot and then letting it fall down. And her face was so sad and strange but also entirely familiar. It was like my CELLS recognized her, so far deep down that it was a feeling instead of even something that I was thinking, and they all just kind of exhaled. Like every part of me had been held so tight and then it wasn't. I saw how sorry she was.

Jedgar, you know what? That isn't really the end. My life story isn't ready to be packaged up yet, with a beginning and middle and end, because this whole thing isn't the end of anything, it is just an in-between bit. I get it now, I think, what Buddha meant. There aren't really endings until you're dead. If you are the river (or the path!), then it just keeps going and going and sometimes it's like basically a trickle and sometimes it's more like Niagara Falls, but it doesn't have ends, it all just blurs together and making it end would be dumb. It just wouldn't make sense, after all.

Anyway, watch the video, OK?

Ruth

Dear Ruth,

It was unbelievably lovely to meet you. It was a *miracle* to meet you. I'm glad you liked the painting. I did so many of the two of you, but that one was special. It was the last one where I painted you both, where I said good-bye. I didn't know I'd get to say 'hello' again. So, hello.

And thank you.

I know I'm not your mum, not really, but I also am. And I know you have to decide how much of me to let into your life, and that's fine. I'm here. I'll be right here. Me and Ruby. Whenever you need us. That doesn't seem like nearly enough, but that's all I can think of to offer you.

Your *SHORCA!* film was brilliantly different and jolly good, actually. The tiny sculptures you made . . . well, it's like you got part of me, after all! Ruby's hopeless at sculpting, but she can draw like an angel. And you? You can sculpt. The two of you, together, are so much like me, but at the same time, so much MORE than me. It's hard to even get my head around the idea that I could have made you, and that you could then be this huge life force. Because you are, Ruth. You are a HUGE life force.

It feels like a miracle, Ruth. It IS a miracle. I hope you know that you're a miracle.

And I hope you know that I'm sorry.

I am. So. Sorry.

Love,

Delilah (Mummy)

FROM: **Ruth Quayle** `iamruthquayle@gmail.com`

TO: **Delilah Starling** `theartistdelilah@yahoo.co.uk`

Dear Delilah,

I think I'll stick with Delilah, if you don't mind. I have a mom already. But seriously, if I was going to call you something else, it would be MUM, not Mummy. Are all of you in cahoots? We are almost 13 years old! You are MUM and MOM. Not Mummy. Not Mommy.

It was really unbelievable to meet you. And thank you for the art. It's still so strange and actually kind of creepy to see a painting of me that isn't actually me because you didn't know me, but there I am, sitting in a park where I've never been, when I was three. It doesn't make sense. It gives me goose bumps, because you thought I was dead when you painted it, so it's a little like I'm looking at a ghost of myself, which is totes creepy.

You can stop saying sorry now. You really can.

It's OK.

I forgive you.

I forgive me.

I forgive all of us for everything that happened.

And it's not enough to say it, but it also is, I guess.

Love,

Ruth

P.S. If you ever want to, I write some poems and stuff like that on a Tumblr at nopoppingballoons.tumblr.com. You do NOT have to read them! Don't feel like you do! Just, you know, because you wrote me that poem before, I thought you might like to read mine.

Ruby to Nan

Dear Nan,

This is it. This is my last letter. I've met Ruth now. So now there's her and me and there's Mum. And that's that. I'm still furious that you did this, that you were the one behind it all, that you decided for all of us how it's going to be.

I'm going to be OK, though. I was just watching the news on the BBC, just like you used to every night, and they had this astronaut they were interviewing. He was up in space! In the Space Station, if you can believe it! It's so strange to me that there are people up there. I'd panic, for sure, to be so far away from earth. But maybe I wouldn't. Maybe I'd like it. Because, after all, it's like living in my wardrobe, but in the stars.

Anyway, he was telling this story of how yesterday, he looked out of his window as they were passing over Australia. He said he looked down, and it looked like a river of rainbows. He saw the Southern Lights, which I suppose are like the Northern Lights, but he was seeing them from above, not from below. He said it was like rainbows were spilling out everywhere, all over the earth.

I loved that, Nan. It made me think of you. Before, I was thinking of you being dead as something you had to break through to come back and spell things on the fridge, but now I think it's not like that. I think it's more like what he said, like rainbows spilling over the earth, and I think those rainbows are you, Nan. I really do. It's like you're here, but only sometimes, just for a few beautiful minutes, and it isn't your job while you're here to do things or to make amends. It's just to remind me of you. And that makes me think that actually, it's silly to think you're reading my letters.

I'm going to let you go now, Nan.

I love you forever. Even though you messed up. I think that's the right thing to do.

Love,

Ruby

Jedgar,

Did you watch it? I wanted you to watch it before I explained it, so now I'll explain it, even though I guess you can guess what happened. Somehow the date we left for England was *also* the date of the Walk to Remember — the walk we do every year with the McNays and all those other people who had a kid who they really loved with their whole hearts who had to go earlier than anyone wanted. I've told you about this. We remember Ashley Mary Jane and write notes and let them go on balloons and listen to people doing speeches about being parents who lost babies, and everyone cries and sings and eats sandwiches and eventually starts to have fun, even though it feels both right and wrong to have fun when you're at a party to say good-bye again to some kids who died when they shouldn't have.

I felt so terrible that we were in *England* for that, because it's all they get, the McNays. That's all that's left of Ashley Mary Jane, letting go of balloons and remembering her. It sort of feels like we all have to do it at once, so the power of that will somehow reach her. That sounds totes ridic, of course, but it's how it feels.

So we made a different arrangement this year and did our walk at the cemetery near the village where Ruby lives. I mean, obviously the McNays weren't there, or any of the other people, but we Skyped it to them even though the time zones were off, so it was the morning for them. We got the perfect rainbow balloons too. Balloons are just better in England! Like everything! Different and better! (And — if you can believe it — specially made so that when they burst, the pieces aren't harmful to wildlife, they just disintegrate!) Everyone wrote a note to Ashley Mary Jane that said "Thank you, Ashley Mary Jane, for Ruth's heart" and things like that. And we all sent them off at once, to the other side of the world. I bet she felt our love more than ever this year in heaven or wherever.

The one bit that I only showed you, on the camera, is that I also wrote a note and sent it off on a different balloon. Only one balloon, all by itself, a blue one. I wrote, "Forgive." It felt like it meant something, even though I don't know who it was meant for. All of us, I guess.

I don't think anyone saw but you. And that's OK. It wasn't for anyone else. Just me. But I knew you'd get it. And when that blue balloon floated up next to all those colorful ones, Jedgar, it was the most beautiful thing I'd ever seen. It was the most amazeballs thing EVER. In a weird way, it was like everything bad and hard and horrible that I'd been feeling floated up with that balloon. I guess, technically, that should make me feel lighter, but I felt more stuck down to the ground than ever. I felt like I was exactly where I was supposed to be.

See you in a couple of days!

Ruth

FROM: **Ruby Starling** starling_girl@mail.com

TO: **Ruth Quayle** iamruthquayle@gmail.com

Ruth,

Are you back home now? You must be, but I think it's night there now. I have a clock on the wall set to your time, so I don't get muddled, and it says it's 1:00, but I don't know if it's 1 in the morning or in the afternoon without figuring it out properly. So if you're sleeping, don't answer this note!

The thing is that when you and Delilah went off to sit on the bench and have a good long chat about everything — I'm sorry she was like that, it's like she suddenly woke up to the idea that you're real and she had to know everything about you right away. Well, anyway, while you were over with her, I wandered away from Fi and the rest of them and down to the river. There weren't any leaves. I was a bit disappointed because it felt like there should be, like that would have been a right ending to our story. I could have thrown them in, but that would have been like cheating a bit somehow, I think. So I sat down and put my feet in. The water was lovely. I put on my iPod and was going to listen to STOP but I changed my mind. I re-read this message I'd got earlier from Fi's cousin Berk. I was looking at my feet, all distorted in the water, thinking, *Now it's starting, this whole thing. I'm going to be 13 soon and maybe Berk will be my first boyfriend.* I felt a bit happy about that, so I was smiling, and that's when I noticed that the Mole had wandered down behind me and was sitting there, just staring at me awkwardly like he does, scratching at his head like maybe he had nits.

But he wasn't, actually. I don't know why I said that about the nits. I suppose that's something that Fi would have said. He said, 'It's cool you have a twin, Ruby, yeah? S'like a film'. And I said, 'It is like that, totally'. But then, Ruth, something funny happened in my stomach, like flapping, like how they say you have butterflies. I think it was his voice. I don't know what it is about it. So anyway, I went and sat next to him. He smelled lovely, actually. Not just like soap and detergent, but something else. Grass. Of course, we were sitting on the grass, so maybe it was just that he smelled summery. Anyway, he said something like, 'School next week then'. And I said, 'Yes'. And he said, 'I like school. I'm good at it'. And I said, 'I expect you are. My sister Ruth is smart too. But I'm better at clothes and things'. And he said, 'Yeah, you always look nice'. And then I said, 'Thanks'. I don't know how it happened, but then we snogged again.

Then he said, 'I'll see you then'. And I said, 'Yes, OK'. Then he got up and walked away.

I sat there for a good bit, watching you in the distance talking to Mum. I guess you could have seen us, if you'd looked up, but you were looking at her the whole time. It felt funny, like I was looking at myself. But anyway, after a while, I opened my messages again and deleted that note from Berk.

I can't explain why I didn't tell you this sooner. It's funny, isn't it, that now we are officially sisters, I felt shy about the snogging. Telling you about it, I mean. Strange, right?

You know what else is strange? Life. One minute you are just plain old you, then suddenly you have a twin in America, or start fancying your best friend's brother, or someone brings the dinosaurs back from extinction, or you look on the Internet one day and see that *SHORCA!* has gone viral. (Which it did. 50,000 hits? That's amazeog. I'd never have thought that 13-year-olds made that.) Or your mum turns out to be so complicated. Or your nan turns out to be someone you didn't think she was. Or you have a very frightening-looking dog who is actually turning out to be your favourite thing ever.

And the thing is that everything overlaps. The important minutes and the not-so-important minutes, and you want to say, 'Wait, don't snog me now, I'm just processing all the minutes that have happened'. As though you expect it all to come in a sequence of digestible bits, like the kibble that Peaches eats. Everything in its own separate compartment. But then it doesn't. It all comes at once in great big rushes, everyone with all their own stories going on, and everything overlapping at once, like tiny silken threads, and it all makes a big picture, do you see? It all makes one big gorgeous, strange, true life.

I have to go. Chlophie and Fi are here and I'm going to take them to the Thrift to buy their school clobber. They are trying to read what I'm writing! Get lost, you lot, it's PRIVATE.

Oh, they want me to tell you that you're *fab* and your teeth are super glam and they're so happy they got to meet you, even if it was just for twelve seconds while you were crying and waving good-bye from the taxicab. They are shouting at me now to ask if they can come and stay if they save enough money to go to America one day, but not to worry, because that'll take them yonks as they're always spending their allowance on nail varnish and nice shoes. OK, CHLOPHIE! I TOLD HER!

And Fi says, 'Hiya'.

Anyway, if you're not sleeping, WRITE BACK RIGHT AWAY, RUTH QUAYLE!

Love,

Ruby

SHORCA!:

The TRUE and TERRIFYING Tale of the
Shark/Orca That Ate Everyone on the Coast of
Oregon and Some People on Washington and
California Beaches, Also

Written and directed by Jedgar Johnston
(with Ruth Quayle)

Show GIRL and BOY racing down the hill to the beach on a hot sunny day to sound track of really great music. BOY trips and scrapes his knee.

BOY: I'm bleeding!
GIRL: It's nothing! Let's go swimming!
BOY: But what if sharks smell blood and attack?

BOY and GIRL look at each other, then fall all over themselves laughing. They run into the water, which is crowded with swimmers and waders.

A fin approaches slowly through the water, then disappears.

GIRL: *(screams)*
BOY: *(screams)*
GIRL: *(screams more)*
BOY: *(screams more)*

SHORCA chomps up BOY and GIRL and several other people (paper drawings) and then burps under-water. Show burp bubbles rising to the music.

VOICE-OVER: BEHOLD, THE SHORCA. THERE IS NOTH-ING ELSE IN THE OCEAN QUITE AS DEADLY — OR AS

SMART—AS THIS BEAST. SHE CAN BE FRIENDLY. SOME DIVERS EVEN SUGGEST SHE'S . . . FUNNY.

Show PAPER DIVERS filming SHORCA frolicking in the deep, doing twirls like a ballerina, sticking her weirdly long tongue out at the camera. Show PAPER DIVERS laughing.

VOICE-OVER: BUT WHEN SHE FEELS LONELY . . .

Show PAPER TEENAGERS looking zitty and slouchy and annoyed, reading THE CATCHER IN THE RYE and being intense. Pull back "camera" to reveal they are at the beach. Show SHORCA flopping up onto the beach. PAPER TEENAGERS scream apathetically. SHORCA eats them before belly flopping back to sea.

VOICE-OVER: FATHERED BY A SHARK WHO DIED SHORTLY AFTER HER BIRTH, AND MOTHERED BY A WHALE WHO ABANDONED HER FOR MYSTERIOUS REASONS, SHE IS UNIQUE. A SPECIES UNTO HERSELF. ALONE IN A WORLD THAT DOESN'T COMPREHEND HER. DOOMED TO A LIFE-TIME OF BEING MISUNDERSTOOD.

Show MAP OF COAST OF AMERICA and trace PATH OF SHORCA. Cut to multiple scenes of SHORCA chomp-ing BEACH PEOPLE. Spinning postcards indicate

*where the SHORCA is currently striking. Back-
ground dialogue is screaming in all different
languages, but mostly English and Spanish.*

VOICE-OVER CONTINUES: LIKE ALL MAMMALS, SHORCAS
CRAVE THE COMPANIONSHIP OF ONE OF THEIR OWN KIND.

*Play sad music as SHORCA searches the deep for
one of her own, and along the way chomps basically every marine mammal that she sees, which
all scream similarly to BEACH PEOPLE in a combi-
nation of different languages.*

VOICE-OVER CONTINUES: AND THEN . . .

*Show GIRL and BOY (similar to first GIRL and BOY
but different) at the beach.*

GIRL: It sure is hot! I wish we could swim.
BOY: But . . . but . . . what about SHORCA?!
GIRL: I miss the water. You know what? I'm going
to dive right in.

*GIRL dives into water. Ominous music. Show BOY
through watery-surface type effect. Show GIRL sur-
facing and swimming and not being chomped.*

BOY: Wow! You weren't chomped!

Show SHORCA rushing toward GIRL — similar fin effect to earlier.

BOY: GET OUT OF THE WATER! THE SHORCA! THE SHORCA!

Show second SHORCA also rushing toward GIRL.

Show both SHORCAs slamming on their brakes, the large wave of water pulling the BOY into the water too.

BOY: Now we will die for sure!

Show the SHORCAs recognizing each other. Play swelling of music as they tap noses and do elaborate fin handshake. SHORCAs spin/dance off into the sunset. The BOY and GIRL get out of the water and sit on the pier, watching the SHORCAs swim away. BOY and GIRL are holding hands.

VOICE-OVER: THE SHORCA, NO LONGER ALONE, NOW FEELS COMPLETE.

THE TWO SHORCAS LIVE IN THE DEEP WATERS OFF AUSTRALIA, WHERE THEY PERFORM FOR TOURISTS.

THE TOURISTS FEED THEM HOT DOGS.

EVERYONE LIKES HOT DOGS.

THE SHORCAS ARE HAPPY.

Camera cuts away from hot dog-eating SHORCAs, uplifting music swells.

Credits roll.

ACKNOWLEDGMENTS

Writing this book has been a huge lesson to me in being both a leaf on a river, and the river itself. Neither thing probably means what I think it means, but I suspect that it means that sometimes you have to just entirely give up control. By giving up my idea of what this book should be, it became what it was meant to be all along, which turned out to be a surprise, even to me. The best kind of surprise. For that, I have to thank my brilliant and ever-patient editors: Cheryl Klein, who consistently wows me with her gentle rerouting of my crazy tributaries, streams, and great crashing waterfalls of (occasionally terrible) ideas; and her Canadian counterpart, the always amazing Sandy Bogart Johnston.

It never ceases to amaze me how many people are involved in the process of taking a book from concept to fruition, and my gratitude to all the people who are hidden behind office doors, working magic, is boundless. I'd name names, but I don't know most of them, and I don't want to miss anyone. So let's just make it a big, all-round, and whole-hearted THANK YOU to the copy editors, the marketing team, the designers, and everyone.

I've been supported over the last decade or so by both the Canada Council for the Arts and the British Columbia Arts Council. The money may have been for other projects, but any and all grants are a vote of confidence that inspires long after the funds run out and the other projects are complete.

My endlessly patient friends who sometimes don't see me or hear from me for months at a time, but are still there when I need them; my always-supportive family; my former agent, Marissa Walsh, and my current agent, Jennifer Laughran; and, of course, all the people in my life from whom I mercilessly steal turns of phrase and lovely accents. Thank you.

As always, for Mum and Dad, and for my two amazing kids: I hope I make you all proud.

And to all my exceptionally wonderful readers: THANK YOU. You can always find me at karenrivers.com and let me know what you thought of the book. I'd be so pleased to hear from you.

Kate, it's your turn to write.

ABOUT THE AUTHOR

Karen Rivers is the author of many wonderful novels for children, teenagers, and adults, including *The Encyclopedia of Me*, in which Ruth Quayle, Jedgar Johnston, and several other characters from this book first appeared. Born in British Columbia, Canada, Karen went to college for ages and ages and studied a little bit of almost everything before she became a writer full-time. She now lives with her family in Victoria, British Columbia, where she loves taking long walks and lots of pictures. Please visit her website at www.karenrivers.com and follow her on Twitter at @karenrivers.

This book was edited by Cheryl Klein and designed by Jeannine Riske. The text was set in Bembo, with display type set in DIN Schrift LT. This book was printed and bound by R. R. Donnelley in Crawfordsville, Indiana. The production was supervised by Starr Baer. The manufacturing was supervised by Shannon Rice.